D1632260

The
IDYLLS
of
THEOCRITUS

Also translated by THELMA SARGENT

THE HOMERIC HYMNS

The IDYLLS *of* THEOCRITUS

A Verse Translation by

THELMA SARGENT

W. W. Norton & Company

New York London

Published simultaneously in Canada by George J. McLeod Limited, Toronto.

Printed in the United States of America

First Edition

The type faces used in this book are Janson with Weiss Initials Series II.
Manufactured by The Maple-Vail Book Manufacturing Group.
Designed by Andrew Roberts.

Library of Congress Cataloging in Publication Data
Theocritus.
The Idylls of Theocritus.
I. Sargent, Thelma. II. Title.
PA4443.E5S2 1982 884'.01 81-9517
ISBN 0-393-01498-3 AACR2
ISBN 0-393-00073-7 (pbk.)

W. W. Norton & Company, Inc. 500 Fifth Avenue, New York, N.Y. 10110
W. W. Norton & Company Ltd. 25 New Street Square, London EC4A 3NT

1 2 3 4 5 6 7 8 9 0

Contents

Foreword

This is a world where shepherds and cowherds and goatherds tend their flocks and herds in the fields and mountains under sunny Mediterranean skies and stop to exchange gossip or to engage in singing contests; where everyone works out of doors, but not very hard; where springs and rivers and nymphs abound and Pan is invoked more often than Zeus; where flowers grow underfoot and trees give welcome shade for noonday rest. There are wolves offstage and dogs to protect the flocks, but no spiders or ants or mosquitoes to trouble suffering mortals. A thorn in the foot is about the worst that can happen to an inhabitant of this world, aside from the usual complications of love.

But the people who live and move in this idealized landscape are real enough—a farmer sick with love for a scrawny flute girl, and the foreman of the reaping gang who shows both humor and practicality in dealing with him; a girl who resorts to magic and incantation to win back a glamorous athlete who has jilted her, with a hint of murder if the spell doesn't work; a Caliban who pines for a sea nymph and woos her with an invitation to help with the milking; the sea nymph herself who gets jealous and sulks when Caliban changes his tactics; a goatherd driven to distraction by a hardhearted maiden who lives in a cave, who gets a headache on top of all his other troubles; a man whose mistress has deserted him for a younger man who thinks of joining the army to get away from it all; two housewives of Alexandria who complain about their husbands' shortcomings and compare notes on the cost of living.

But through all this woe and heartache is heard the affectionate laughter of the poet, who clearly found his fellow human beings both lovable and comical. He even laughs at himself.

The idylls (the word means "short pieces") fall roughly into four groups: the pastoral (or bucolic) poems, with the shepherds and their singing contests; vignettes of city or country life, a love poem, and the two formal addresses (Idd. 16 and 17); short epics; and three experiments in the Aeolic dialect (Idd. 28–30). The traditional order of the poems, dating from the sixteenth century, has a certain logic, but the arrangement is not chronological and tells us nothing about the artistic development of Theocritus. Idylls 1 and 2 are obviously not the work of a beginner. (The eight poems in the collection that are now known not to be by Theocritus are indicated by brackets around the titles in the Contents and text.)

Idylls 15, 16, and 17 must have been written between 275 and 270 B.C.—after Hiero II of Syracuse had achieved military fame but before he ascended the throne, and before the death of Queen Arsinoë II of Egypt—but beyond that there is no way of dating the poems. (Ptolemy II Philadelphus became king of Egypt in 285 B.C. at the age of twenty-four, but how close he was in age to Theocritus is not known.) My guess is that the poet moved from pastoral to vignette, with Idyll 7 overlapping the two groups; then to epic, with Idyll 13 the transitional one; and finally to Aeolic, harking back to the vignette in subject matter. He doesn't seem very comfortable in the epic area, though he often echoes Homer and knew him well, and Heracles, the Dioscuri, Helen, and Dionysos may have been distasteful duties, either for the sake of pleasing Ptolemy and justifying his patronage, or to hold his own with the rest of the literary circle in third-century Alexandria.

Theocritus was very much a poet of his age in his use of dactylic hexameter—the dignified six-foot meter of Homer's great poems about the Trojan war and the wanderings of Odysseus—and in the overuse of arcane allusions. This ornamentation is partly because of the nature of the hexameter. It is a long line and has to be filled out somehow, and the Alexandrians made it more complicated by refining the rules. Homer, who was content with "loud-roaring sea," "starry heaven," and "rosy-fingered dawn," would never have fitted in with the crowd in Alexandria, though the sea, the sky, and the dawn had changed in no way for the last five hundred—or fifty thousand—years. The Alexandrian poets shied away from the obvious, and since they were writing for each other, they liked to show off their erudition. The great controversy of the time was over the length of a poem. Theocritus sided with Callimachus, who favored short poems—an epic subject, but some out-of-the-way aspect of it elaborately handled and highly polished—and in "Hylas" (Id. 13) and "The Dioscuri" (Id. 22) he scored over Apollonius Rhodius, whose long epic *The Argonauts* (in four books) also treats of those incidents. (There is no certainty about which version came first, but there is no doubt that Theocritus wrote better poetry.)

Theocritus was anything but conventional in his use of words. He seemed to love experimenting with them, and often used them to mean something they hadn't meant before, and sometimes even invented completely new ones. In fact, he sometimes gives the impression of becoming so fascinated with novelty that he loses track of what he's saying. In "Hylas," for example, after the heroes have gone to great pains to cut down meadow grasses to prepare their bed for the night, they take to their ship again around midnight. In another place, the word meaning "big," conventionally applied to Telamonian Ajax, is transferred to Achilles in the same line, and the adjective describing Ajax is a word that could mean either "overweight" or "boring"—neither very appropriate in a heroic context, though once Hector called him an "inarticulate ox." Whether in the great Library at Alexandria Theocritus had access to mythological accounts we have no knowledge of is not certain, but his version of the fight between Castor and Lynceus in Idyll 22, for example, does not tally with any of the accounts we do have. Castor too was killed in the fight, and it was over sharing the spoils of a cattle raid, and anyway Idas was already married to Marpessa. It is perfectly possible that he made up myths out of his imagination just for the fun of it. He was not a librarian or grammarian, as both Callimachus and Apollonius were, and probably cared more about words and their marvelous ways than about facts and logic.

While he wrote mostly in his native Doric dialect—the kind of Greek spoken in Syracuse, his birthplace, and in Cos, where he lived for a number of years before going to Alexandria—he often used Ionic, Attic, and epic words and sometimes a different dialect for a whole poem. In Idylls 28–30 he experimented with Aeolic, the dialect of Sappho and Alcaeus, and tried out other meters as well—a matter of syllables, but since the hexameter varies from twelve to seventeen syllables, the difference is not striking.

But the pastoral poem itself is the great novelty for which Theocritus is famous. The world of shepherds and music and love and beauty struck a responsive chord in the human heart that has reverberated down through the ages—a longing for escape, for the simple life close to nature, free of the complexities of civilization and tribulations of daily life.* The eight anonymous idylls in the collection were early imitations, most of them so good they were thought for a long time to be by Theocritus himself. Bion and Moschus, who probably lived in the second century B.C., and a pupil of Bion's who wrote the famous "Lament for Bion" are also good and are usually lumped together with Theocritus as "The Bucolics." Virgil's *Eclogues*, though he selected and rearranged to suit his own purposes, are sometimes very close imitations—the sorceress of Idyll 2 appears again, with a different spell, in a singing contest in Eclogue 8, and the Gallus of Eclogue 10 bears more than a casual resemblance to the Daphnis of Idyll 1. Virgil's

* The simple life close to nature is, of course, far from "idyllic" and is what the mass of mankind has always longed to escape *from*.

lines are often very beautiful, but the special something that breathed life into the original Daphnis and Lycidas and Corydon and Amaryllis is missing.

So it has been ever since, in all languages and all countries. Many great poets, some far more profound, have followed where Theocritus led, and though the shepherds and flutes and nymphs and landscapes are often lovely—as in Milton's "Lycidas" and Arnold's "Thyrsis"—and though Shakespeare added a touch of reality to *As You Like It* with Adam and Corin, they are not quite the same. There is an artificiality that is inherent in the pastoral—because after all it is a dream world, a fairyland—but the inventor came closest to making it real and he has never been surpassed.

All that we know about his life must be inferred from the idylls themselves. He was a native of Syracuse, a Greek city in eastern Sicily, and according to one not necessarily reliable bit of external evidence—a four-line epigram written in the first person but now thought to be by an editor of the first century B.C.—his parents were Praxagoras and Philinna, and his mother is described as "very famous." They are thought to have been of Coan birth or descent. He lived in Cos* for a number of years, but whether his whole family moved there or whether he went off as a youth to further his education is not known. While he was in Cos he may have studied under Philitas, an outstanding poet of the day who was also the tutor of Ptolemy Philadelphus, and it may have been in Cos that he met Nicias, who may have been a student at the great medical school there. In 275 B.C. he wrote Idyll 16, seeking patronage from Hiero II of Syracuse, his home town, but apparently did not get it. How old he was at the time is not known, but *if* he was born in 300 B.C. he would have been twenty-five, which seems reasonable to me, and therefore fifteen when Ptolemy

* An island in the southeastern Aegean Sea off the southwestern coast of Caria (modern Turkey), not far from the Dorian cities of Halicarnassos and Cnidos; the birthplace of Hippocrates, the great physician of antiquity, and Ptolemy II Philadelphus, king of Egypt from 285 to 246 B.C.

Philadelphus became king, or nine years younger than Ptolemy. He is in Alexandria very shortly after the poem to Hiero, and may have been there for some time. He visits Nicias and his wife in Miletos, where Nicias is practicing medicine, and presents an ivory distaff of Syracusan workmanship to Nicias's wife, but we do not know when he made the voyage or what city he sailed from. It may have been on this occasion that he wrote an inscription for a statue of Asclepios Nicias had commissioned. (In addition to the idylls and a couple of fragments, there are twenty-five or so epigrams and a pattern poem that are usually attributed to Theocritus—his complete poetic work as far as we know.) He seems not himself to have married, but his domestic touches in Idylls 15 and 24 make one wonder, and in Idyll 7, thought to be autobiographical, as Simichidas he starts off his song with a reference to his own normal love for a girl. Still, Idylls 12, 29, and 30 are concerned with love for a boy. His hair is getting white in Idylls 14 and 30, and in 260 B.C. he would have been forty. In view of his limited output, it is not unreasonable to think he may have died young. But it is an area in which speculation abounds, and the few facts can be arranged to fit almost any theory.

I have followed the text of A. S. F. Gow in *Bucolici Graeci* (Oxford University Press, 1952; 1962 printing) and have relied heavily on his *Theocritus* (Cambridge University Press, 1950; 1965 printing), especially his invaluable commentary in Volume II. The Loeb edition of J. M. Edmonds, *The Greek Bucolic Poets* (London: Heinemann, 1912; 1970 printing), has also been very helpful.

I hope the charm and humor of Theocritus have not completely vanished in a language so different from the one in which he took such delight. I have tried to be as faithful to his words as to his spirit, but even when his meaning is perfectly clear—as it often is not—it creates problems in English. Why should a man whose interest in botany is more than superficial and who is unusually observant describe celandine as "blue" and cypresses as having "leaves at the top"—both nonsensical?

Because he was having a pleasant alliterative play on *kappa* in one case and a combination of *kappa* and *chi* in the other. But all a translator can do is ignore the cleverness where it won't work in English and try to get it in somewhere else. I have used a rather flexible line roughly corresponding to the rhythm of the hexameter, but have made no attempt to reproduce the Aeolic meters. The transliteration is of the Greek variety, but not consistently so. Where the Latin form is familiar—for example, the author's name and "Aeolic" in a literary context—I have used that form, and "c" instead of "k" simply because it looks better to me in English.

The Glossary is for the convenience of readers who are curious about where Mytilene is or who Endymion or Teiresias were. The footnotes are limited to explaining the mysterious references that more or less matter, and to textual information.

And now, which idyll to start with? Almost everyone likes "The Sorceress" (Id. 2), "The Harvest Festival" (Id. 7), and "The Adonis Festival" (Id. 15). I myself am also fond of "Cyclops" (Id. 11).

T. S.

New York City
March 1980

1

Song of Thyrsis

THYRSIS

Sweet is the whisper of wind as it plays in that pine
Near the spring, O goatherd, and sweet, too, is your piping;
In a contest with Pan you would win second prize.
If he took the horned he-goat, you'd win the dam,
But should his prize be the dam, the kid would be yours,
And a kid before it gives milk is delectable eating.

GOATHERD

Sweeter, O shepherd, pours forth the song from your lips
Than the water tumbling down from those rocks overhead.
Should the Muses bear away a ewe as their gift,
The cosset lamb would be your prize; but if the lamb
Should content them, you next would be awarded the ewe.

THYRSIS

By the nymphs, goatherd, would it please you to sit down
On this sloping hillock here where the tamarisks grow
And play your syrinx,* while I meanwhile look after your
goats?

GOATHERD

Custom forbids, O shepherd, that at noontime we play on the
syrinx,
For we go in fear of great Pan. At this time of day,
Weary, he rests from the chase. He has an irascible temper,
And bitter gall perches forever over his nostrils.

* The panpipe. In Theocritus's time the reeds were of equal length with wax stops to produce the different tones.

But you, Thyrsis, sing of the sorrows of Daphnis
And are skilled in the pastoral song of the Muses.
Let us sit down here under the elm tree facing Priapos
And the nymphs of the spring, where stand the oaks
And the bench of the shepherds, and if you sing as you did
When vying in song once with Chromis of Libya,
I will let you have a twin-bearing goat for three milkings,
Who, besides feeding two kids, yields up to two milk pails,
And a deep ivywood drinking cup coated with sweet-scented
wax,
Two-handled and newly wrought, and from the chisel still
fragrant.
Ivy twines high along the lip of the cup,
And scattered among the ivy leaves are helichryse blossoms,
And the spiraling tendrils below are glorious with golden fruit.
Inside the cup is a woman, carved as by one of the gods,
Wearing a peplos* and headband; two men stand beside her
With fine long hair, contending with speeches, first one,
Then the other in turn, but they cannot kindle her heart.
At one moment, laughing, she looks on this man,
The next moment turns her mind to the other, while they,
Long heavy-eyed from love's suffering, labor in vain.
Near them is engraved a fisherman on a rough rock,
An old man who visibly strains as he gathers up
His great net for a cast, like a man worn out with hard work.
You might say he was fishing with all the strength of his limbs
From the swollen sinews that stand out all over his neck,
But gray-haired though he is, his strength is that of a youth.
And not far away from this seaworn old man is a vineyard
Heavily laden with ripening clusters of grapes,
Where on a dry-stone wall a small boy sits on guard.

* A woman's full outer garment.

Two foxes flank him: one prowls up and down the vine rows,
Pilfering the already ripe fruit, while the other
Directs all her cunning toward the boy's wallet, and vows not to
rest
Until she has left him lean fare for his breakfast.
But he, plaiting with asphodel stalks a fine cage for locusts,
Fits in a reed and thinks not at all of his wallet
Or of the vines, so great is his joy in his weaving.
And all over the cup is spread the wavy acanthus—
A sight for goatherds! The marvelous thing will amaze you!
I gave the Calydnian boatman a she-goat in payment
And a great wheel of white cheese. Never so far
Has it been touched by my lips, but still lies unsullied.
It would be a pleasure indeed, my friend, to give it to you
If you would sing for me that beautiful song.
I do not mock you. Come, sir, for to hoard it
Will not serve you at all in Hades' realm where all is forgotten.

THYRSIS

Begin the pastoral song, dear Muses, begin the song.

Thyrsis of Etna am I, and this is the sweet voice of Thyrsis.
Where were you, nymphs, where were you when Daphnis was
wasting?
In Tempe, the lovely vale of Peneios, or off on the slopes of the
Pindos?
For not then did you haunt the great stream of the river Anapos
Or Etna's high peak or the holy waters of Acis.

Begin the pastoral song, dear Muses, begin the song.

For him the jackals lamented, for him the wolves howled,
For him, dead, the lion mourned in the oak wood.

Begin the pastoral song, dear Muses, begin the song.

Around him cows without number and bulls made lament,
Many a heifer and many a calf too bewailed him.

Begin the pastoral song, dear Muses, begin the song.

Hermes came from the hill first of all and said, "Daphnis,
Who wastes away your life thus? For whom, good man, such
desire?"

Begin the pastoral song, dear Muses, begin the song.

The cowherds came, the shepherds came, and the goatherds,
And all of them asked why he suffered. Priapos came too
And said, "Daphnis, poor wretch, why are you pining? The girl
On hastening feet goes to every spring, every grove searching.

Begin the pastoral song, dear Muses, begin the song.

"A laggard in love are you and helpless indeed!
Cowherd you were called, but now you resemble a goatherd—
A goatherd, forsooth, who when he sees nannies mounted
Pines, teary-eyed, because he was not born a he-goat.

Begin the pastoral song, dear Muses, begin the song.

"And you, whenever you chance to see maidens laughing,
Pine, teary-eyed, because you cannot dance among them."
To all of this the herdsman made no reply,
But endured his bitter love, bore it out to the end preordained.

Begin the song, Muses, begin again the pastoral song.

Cypris came too, sweetly laughing but laughing falsely,
Holding back the wrath deep in her heart,
And said, "Daphnis, you vowed to wrestle Love to a fall,
But have not you yourself been thrown by mischievous Eros?"

Begin the song, Muses, begin again the pastoral song.

And to her then Daphnis replied, "Hardhearted Cypris,
Cypris the terrible, Cypris hateful to mortals,
Are you so sure that all my suns have already set?
Even in Hades will Daphnis be bitter trouble for Eros.

Begin the song, Muses, begin again the pastoral song.

"Is it not said that with Cypris a cowherd once—? Creep off to
Ida,
Crawl to Anchises; oak trees grow there and galingale,
And bees murmurously hum in swarms round the hives.

Begin the song, Muses, begin again the pastoral song.

"Adonis, too, in the prime of his youth pastures his flocks,
And shoots hares and hunts every wild beast in the chase.

Begin the song, Muses, begin again the pastoral song.

"Or go take up your stand again before Diomedes
And say, 'I overcame Daphnis the herdsman, but come on and
fight me.'

Begin the song, Muses, begin again the pastoral song.

"O wolves, O jackals, O bears lurking in dens in the mountains,
Farewell. No more will I, Daphnis the herdsman, pass through
your forest,
No more through your oak woods or groves. Farewell,
Arethusa,
And rivers whose rushing water pours down from Thybris.

Begin the song, Muses, begin again the pastoral song.

"I, that Daphnis who here pastured his cattle,
The Daphnis who here watered his bulls and his calves.

Begin the song, Muses, begin again the pastoral song.

"O Pan, Pan, whether you range the lofty peaks of Lycaios
Or busy yourself on high Mainalos, come to the island
Of Sicily, leaving Helike's mound and the tall tomb
Of the son* of Lycaon's daughter,† at which even the blessed
ones marvel.

Cease the song, Muses, cease now the pastoral song.

* Arcas, ancestor of the Arcadians.
† Helike, or Callisto, mother of Arcas by Zeus.

"Come, lord, and take this sweet-breathing syrinx smelling of honey
And beeswax, and bound securely around the fine lip,
For now, defeated by Eros, I go down to Hades.

Cease the song, Muses, cease now the pastoral song.

"Now you brambles, you thornbushes, may you bear violets,
May the lovely narcissus on junipers bloom,
Let all be confounded, and pears grow on pine trees,
Since Daphnis is dying; may deer drag down dogs,
And may owls from the mountains to nightingales sing."

Cease the song, Muses, cease now the pastoral song.

So much he said, then was silent. Willingly would Aphrodite
Have spared him but the whole thread of his fate had run out,
And Daphnis went to the stream.* The swirling waters washed over
The man dear to the Muses, the man not abhorred by the nymphs.

Cease the song, Muses, cease now the pastoral song.

Now give me the goat and the cup, so I may milk her
And pour out to the Muses an offering. Muses, farewell,
Many times farewell, but I will sing you a sweeter song later.

GOATHERD

May your lovely mouth be filled with honey, Thyrsis,
Filled too with honeycomb, and may you munch the sweet figs
Of Aigilia, for you sing to surpass the cicada.
See, here is the cup; notice, my friend, its fine fragrance.
It would make you think it was dipped in the spring of the Hours.
Come here, Cissaitha!—you milk her. Don't frisk around,
You other nannies! Calm down lest the billy goat mount you.

* Of Acheron.

2
The Sorceress

Where are my bay leaves? Bring them, Thestylis, and the
love charms,
And wreathe the caldron with fine crimson wool,
That I may bind to myself that man I love, cruel though he be.
For the twelfth day now the wretch has not come to my house,
Nor does he know if I am dead or alive, or, heartless one,
Rattle my door. Surely to some other love he has gone,
His fickle heart in thrall to Aphrodite and Eros.
To Timagetos' wrestling school I will go in the morning
And see him and reproach him for the way that he treats me;
But now I will bind him fast to me with a spell, and, Selene,
Shine brightly, for I will softly sing to you, goddess,
And to Hecate under the earth, before whom whelps tremble
As she comes up through the tombs of the dead and the black
blood.
Hail, terrible Hecate! Attend me to the end,
That this charm may work no worse than any of Circe's
Or those of Medea or yellow-haired Perimede.

Spin, magic wheel, and draw that man to my house.

Let barley first be consumed in the fire. Scatter it,
Thestylis! Wretched girl, where have your wits flown to?
Or have I become, horrid creature, a laughingstock even to you?
Sprinkle it, saying these words: "The bones of Delphis I
scatter."

Spin, magic wheel, and draw that man to my house.

Delphis has wronged me; for Delphis I burn this laurel.
How loudly it crackles as it catches fire,
And, suddenly blazing up, leaves no ash behind it.
So in flame may Delphis's flesh be completely destroyed.

Spin, magic wheel, and draw that man to my house.

This wax I now melt with the goddess's aid;
So may Delphis the Myndian melt at once under love;
And as by Aphrodite's power spins this whirling bronze shape,
So may he irresistibly spin to my door.

Spin, magic wheel, and draw that man to my house.

Now I will offer the bran. And, Artemis, you who can move
Even the adamant gates of Hades, and whatever else is
unyielding—
Thestylis, the dogs howl through the city!
The goddess is at the triple crossways! Sound the bronze
quickly!

Spin, magic wheel, and draw that man to my house.

Look: the sea lies in silence; the winds too are hushed;
But the torment within my breast is not still.
I am all on fire for that man who has made me so wretched
And left me not only no wife but no longer a virgin.

Spin, magic wheel, and draw that man to my house.

Three times do I pour out wine to you, mistress, and three
times I cry:
Whether it is a woman who lies with him now or a man,
May he forget his love as thoroughly as once they say
Theseus on Dia forgot lovely-haired Ariadne.

Spin, magic wheel, and draw that man to my house.

In Arcadia there is a plant called horse-madness, and for it
All of the colts and swift horses go mad on the mountains;

May I see Delphis in just such a frenzy
Come to this house from his oily wrestling arena.

Spin, magic wheel, and draw that man to my house.

Here is a fringe Delphis once lost from his cloak,
And I now, shredding it, throw it into the ravening fire.
Oh, unfeeling Eros, why do you cling to me thus,
Like some leech of the marsh, drinking all the dark blood from
my body?

Spin, magic wheel, and draw that man to my house.

Tomorrow I'll grind up a lizard and send him a poisonous brew,
But now, Thestylis, take these herbs to his house
And smear them high up on his doorposts, while it's still night,
And mutter meanwhile: "The bones of Delphis I splatter."

Spin, magic wheel, and draw that man to my house.

Now I am alone whence shall I weep for this love?
Where should I begin? Who brought this trouble upon me?
As basket-bearer, our servant Anaxo, Eubolos' daughter,
Went to Artemis' grove, and to honor the goddess that day
There was a procession of many wild beasts, a lioness among
them.

Consider whence, mistress Selene, this love of mine came.

And Theumaridas' Thracian nurse—blessed soul, now
departed—
Who was living next door, begged and implored me to go
And watch the procession. And I, most wretched of women,
Accompanied her, trailing a beautiful gown of fine linen,
Clearista's magnificent cloak gathered around me.

Consider whence, mistress Selene, this love of mine came.

When halfway along the highway leading past Lycon's,
I saw Delphis and Eudamippos walking together,
The beards on their faces more golden than helichryse blossoms,

Their breasts gleaming even more brightly, Selene, than you,
For they had just come away from the gym and their manly
exertions.

Consider whence, mistress Selene, this love of mine came.

I went mad when I saw him; my unlucky heart caught on fire,
My looks faded away. I had no further thought
For that procession, and how I got home again I don't know.
But I was suddenly shaken by some parching fever,
And forced to lie abed for ten days and ten nights.

Consider whence, mistress Selene, this love of mine came.

And oftentimes my skin grew as yellow as fustic,
And all my hair began to fall out of my head;
What was left of me was just skin and bones. To whom didn't I
go?
What old crone's house did I not seek out if she knew magic?
But nothing gave me relief, and time was fast flying.

Consider whence, mistress Selene, this love of mine came.

And so I finally told my slave girl the truth.
"Come, Thestylis, find me some cure for this tiresome illness.
The Myndian, alas, altogether possesses my soul.
Go and keep watch at Timagetos' palaestra,*
For he frequents the place, and finds it pleasant to sit there.

Consider whence, mistress Selene, this love of mine came.

"And when you know he is alone, secretly give him a nod
And say, 'Simaitha summons you'; then bring him here."
So I said. And she went and brought Delphis, all shiny of skin,
To my house. But as soon as I was aware
Of his light step at my door as he crossed the threshold—

Consider whence, mistress Selene, this love of mine came—

* A wrestling arena.

I grew colder than snow all over, and from my forehead
Beads of sweat streamed down like wet dew;
Not a word could I say, not even so much as the whimper
Children make in sleep calling for their dear mother,
But my whole beautiful body froze as stiff as a doll's.

Consider whence, mistress Selene, this love of mine came.

He glanced at me, heartless brute, and with his eyes fixed on the
ground,
Sat down on the couch and, sitting there, uttered these words:
"Truly, Simaitha, your calling me to your house
Outdistanced my coming by only so much as I
Not long ago outdistanced in running the charming Philinos.

Consider whence, mistress Selene, this love of mine came.

"For I would have come—yes, by sweet Eros, I would have
come—
With two friends or three just as soon as night fell,
Bearing apples of Dionysos within the folds of my tunic,
And on my head a garland of Heracles' sacred white poplar,
The spray wound all about with bands of deep crimson.

Consider whence, mistress Selene, this love of mine came.

"And if you had received me, that would have been pleasant
(For I am known among all the young men for my swiftness and
beauty),
And I would have slept if I had but kissed your beautiful lips;
But if you had sent me away and put up the bar on your door,
Then axes and torches would have come promptly against you.

Consider whence, mistress Selene, this love of mine came.

"But now I declare I owe my thanks first to Cypris,
And after Cypris, dear lady, to you, for you snatched me,
Already half consumed, out of the fire

By calling me here to your home; for very often
Eros kindles a hotter blaze than Hephaistos on Lipara,

Consider whence, mistress Selene, this love of mine came.

"And with ruinous madness drives the maid from her virginal chamber
And the bride from her bridegroom's bed while it's still warm."
So he spoke. And I, one all too quickly persuaded,
Took his hand and pulled him down beside me upon the soft couch.
And soon body warmed against body and faces glowed
With more heat than before, and we whispered sweetly together.
So as not to babble on about love for too long, Selene,
All came about, and we both assuaged our desire.
And until yesterday he had no fault to find with me,
Nor I with him. But early today, at the time
When her chariot bears rosy Eos swiftly to heaven from Ocean,
The mother of Melixo and of Philista our flute girl
Came and told me among other things that Delphis had fallen in love.
Whether his passion was for a woman or for a man
She claimed not exactly to know, but only this: Always to Eros
He poured out unmixed libations, and afterward
Left in a rush, vowing to deck that house with bright garlands.
So my guest told me, and I believe she is truthful.
He used to come to my house three or four times a day,
And often left in my keeping his Dorian oil flask,
But now it has been twelve days since I have seen him.
Must he not have another sweetheart that he forgets me?
But now I will bind him with a spell, and if he still grieves me,
Then—yes, by the Fates!—may he knock at the entrance of Hades!

For I keep lethal drugs of that sort, I swear, in my casket for
him,
Having learned this lore, mistress, from an Assyrian stranger.
But farewell to you, lady; turn your colts back toward Ocean,
And I will endure my longing as I have endured it.
Farewell, bright-throned Selene, and farewell to you other
Stars, attendants upon the car of calm Night.

3

Serenade

I will serenade Amaryllis while my goats
Browse on the hillside and Tityros tends them.
Tityros, my fine friend, pasture the goats,
And take them to the spring, Tityros, and that he-goat,
That yellowish Libyan hellion, take care lest he butt you!

O lovely Amaryllis, why do you no longer peek out of your cave
And call me, your sweetheart, inside? Do you then really hate me?
Do I appear snub-nosed to you, dear, when you're near me?
Does my beard jut out? I'll hang myself if you say so!
Look! I bring you ten apples. I gathered them
Where you bade me, and I'll bring you others tomorrow.
Do look! Oh, this anguish cuts to my heart! Would that I were
A buzzing bee to slip through the ivy and ferns
That conceal you and find my way into your cave.
Now I know Eros, that terrible god. By a lioness
He was suckled, and his mother raised him in the deep forest,
And the torment of his slow fire pierces me to my bones.
O sweet-glancing nymph, all of stone, O dark-browed maiden,
Come to the arms of your goatherd so I may kiss you,
For even in empty kisses is there sweet gladness.
You'll make me tear to shreds this garland I wear,

This wreath I made in your honor, dear Amaryllis,
Of ivy entwined with rosebuds and sweet-smelling parsley.

Oh, what will become of me, poor beggar? You won't even
listen!

I will strip off my goatskin and throw myself into the sea
From the cliff where Olpis the fisherman watches for tuna,
And if I should die, how could I add to your pleasure?
I knew it before when I wondered whether you loved me,
And the love-in-absence didn't stick when I smacked it
But shriveled up tamely on my smooth forearm.
And Agroio, the sieve-diviner, at the time
She was gathering herbs at my side, told me the truth:
That though I was wholly yours, you thought nothing of me.
I have been saving for you a white goat with twin kids,
Which Mermnon's swarthy servingmaid also begs of me,
And I will give it to her since you treat me so lightly.
My right eye twitches; am I going to see her?
I will step aside under this pine tree and sing for a while,
And she may look at me, for she is not adamantine.

Hippomenes, when he wished to marry the maiden,
Took apples in his hand while running the race,
And Atalanta went mad when she saw them and plunged deep
into love.
And Melampus the seer led the herd from Othrys
To Pylos, and in Bias' embrace at last lay
The charming mother of wise Alphesiboia.
And did not Adonis, pasturing sheep in the mountains,
Drive beautiful Cytherea to such a frenzy
That even in death she puts him not away from her breast?
Enviable to me is Endymion, abiding in unchanging sleep,

And enviable, too, dear lady,* do I consider Iasion,
Whose fate was such as profane ones will never know.

My head aches, but what do you care? I'll sing no more.
I'll lie here where I've fallen, and the wolves will devour me,
And as sweet to you as honey in your throat may it be.

* Demeter.

4

The Herdsmen

BATTOS

Tell me, Corydon, whose cattle are those? Philondas's?

CORYDON

No, Aigon's. He gave them to me to pasture.

BA: And at evening do you milk them all on the sly?

CO: No, the old man puts the calves to their mothers and keeps me under his eye.

BA: And to what part of the world has their herdsman now vanished?

CO: Haven't you heard? Milon has taken him off to the Alpheus.*

BA: When did that one ever set eyes on an oil flask?

CO: They say he rivals Heracles in power and strength.

BA: My mother told me I outranked Polydeuces.

CO: And he went off with a mattock and twenty sheep.

BA: Milon might as well at once persuade the wolves to go mad.

CO: And the heifers miss him—hear how they bellow!

BA: Miserable creatures, they found themselves a poor herdsman.

CO: Miserable indeed! They care no more about grazing.

BA: Certainly there's nothing left of that beast over there but her bones.

Does she breakfast on dewdrops, perhaps, like the cicada?

CO: Lord, no! Sometimes I pasture her by the Aisaros,

And give her tender tussocks to feed on,

* That is, to compete as a boxer at the Olympic games; digging was part of an athlete's training, and the sheep his rations for thirty days.

And other times she frisks on shady Latymnon.

BA: The red bull is lean, too. May the people of Lampriadas
Find such a one when they sacrifice to Hera,
For that whole district is infested with rascals.

CO: But the bull, too, is led to the marsh and to Physcos's
And to the Neaithos, where all good things grow—
Goatwort and fleabane and sweet-smelling balsam.

BA: Alas, alas, wretched Aigon, your herd of cattle will perish
As well because you lust after a trumpery triumph,
And the syrinx you once made is now speckled with mildew.

CO: Not so, by the nymphs! When he went off to Pisa
He bequeathed it to me. I too am a fair musician,
And can play quite well the tunes of Glaucë or Pyrrhos.
I sing the praises of Croton—O beautiful town of Zacynthos!—
Where the shrine of Lacinia faces the dawn, and where the
boxer
Aigon all alone devoured eighty loaves.
There it was too that he seized the bull by the hoof
And led it down the mountain to give Amaryllis,
And the women gave a loud shriek and the herdsman bellowed
with laughter.

BA: O lovely Amaryllis! Even in death
Are you alone not forgotten. As dear as my goats to me
Were you when you died. Alas that so hard a fate should be
mine!

CO: You must take heart, dear Battos. Things may be better
tomorrow.
For the living there is hope, but no hopes have the dead,
And Zeus ordains clear skies at one time and another time rain.

BA: I'm cheerful enough. Drive the calves up from below;
They're nibbling the shoots on the olive trees, the vandals.

CO: Hey you, Lepargos, Cymaitha! Up on the hill, do you hear me?
You'll come to a bad end in a hurry, by Pan you will,

If you don't get out of there! Look at her sneaking right back
again!
If I had a stout crook, I'd give you a hiding!
BA: Look at me, Corydon, for the love of Zeus! A thorn
Has just jabbed me here under the ankle. These spindle thorns
Are thick hereabouts. Devil take that fool calf!
It was while I was gawking at her I was stuck—do you see it?
CO: Yes, and I've got it gripped in my nails. Here it is!
BA: What a small wound to master so large a man!
CO: You shouldn't go barefoot, Battos, when you come to the
mountain,
For on the hill prickly bushes and thistles abound.
BA: But tell me now, Corydon, does that little old lecher
Still hammer that dark-skinned wench he once had an itch for?
CO: Of course, you dolt! Only yesterday as I passed by
The stables did I happen upon him hard at it.
BA: Well done, you old cock! That line closely resembles
The offspring of the satyrs and spindle-shanked Pans.

5

Goatherd and Shepherd

COMATAS

Flee, my goats, from that shepherd, Lacon of Sybaris.
Yesterday he stole my goatskin, the villain.

LACON

Away from the spring—hasten, my lambs! Don't you see
Comatas, who the other day stole my syrinx?

CO: What syrinx? When did you, slave of Sibyrtas,
Own a syrinx? And why are you no longer content
To tootle away with Corydon on your reed whistles?

LA: The one Lycon gave me, O Freeman. But what goatskin of yours
Did Lacon ever make off with? Tell me that, Comatas,
For not even your master Eumaras has one to sleep in.

CO: The spotted one Crocylos gave me when he sacrificed
The goat to the nymphs. And you, you blackhearted viper,
Were envious then, and now at last leave me naked.

LA: Not I, by Pan of the seashore! Lacon the son of Calaithis
Did not divest you of your goatskin. Otherwise, man,
May I go raving mad and jump off that rock into the Crathis.

CO: Neither, good fellow, by these nymphs of the lake—
May they be well disposed and gracious to me—
Did Comatas ever lay a thieving hand on your syrinx.

LA: If I am convinced, may Daphnis's pains fall upon me.
But if you're willing to wager a kid—there's nothing sacred about it—
I'll sing a match with you till you're exhausted.

CO: The pig once challenged Athene. All right, there's my stake—

The kid—but you'll have to put up a fat lamb against it.
LA: And how then, you fox, will it be even between us?
Who would sooner shear hair than wool? And who, a she-goat
With her firstborn at hand, would want to milk a foul bitch?
CO: Whoever is as sure as you are of besting his neighbor—
A buzzing wasp against a cicada. But if the kid
Seems to you an uneven bet, here's this he-goat. Now start the
contest.
LA: Don't be in a hurry. You're not on fire. You'll sing more sweetly
Sitting over here in this grove under the wild olive tree.
Cold water pours down just beyond, grass grows underfoot,
The rushes are pleasant, and locusts are chirping.
CO: I'm in no hurry, but I'm surprised that you dare
Look me straight in the face, I who taught you when you
Were yet a child. See what benevolence comes to—
Raise wolf cubs, raise puppies for them to devour you.
LA: When do I remember learning or hearing anything good
From you, you envious, uncouth little man?
CO: That time I poked you in the rump and you hurt, and these she-
goats
Were bleating, and the billy goat bored them.
LA: No deeper than that pole, hunchback, may you be buried!
But no matter. Come over here and sing your last match.
CO: No, not over there. Here there are oak trees and galingale,
Here the soothing hum of bees round the beehives,
Here two springs of cold water, and in the trees
Birds twitter, and the shade is in every way better
Than where you are, and the pine tree throws its cones down
from above.
LA: Lambskins and sheep's wool softer than sleep shall you tread on
If you come here, but those goatskins
You have over there stink worse than you do.
And I will set out a large bowl of white milk

For the nymphs, and another one of sweet oil.

CO: But if you come over here, you shall tread tender ferns
And pennyroyal blossoms, and you shall lie upon goatskins
Four times as soft as those lambskins of yours.
And I will set out for Pan eight buckets of milk
And eight bowls of honey still in the comb.

LA: Stay where you are, then, and sing against me from there,
Treading your own domain and keeping your oaks.
But who will judge us? If only the cowherd Lycopas should
chance to come by.

CO: I can do without him. But, if you want,
We can call that man over there—the woodsman near you
Who's cutting the heather. Oh, but it's Morson!

LA: Let's give him a yell.

CO: You call him.

LA: Hoy, neighbor! Come here
And listen a bit, for we are having a match to decide
Who is the better pastoral singer. But, Morson, good fellow,
Neither out of kindness judge in my favor nor yet favor him.

CO: Yes, by the nymphs, dear Morson, neither completely
Lean toward Comatas nor be partial to Lacon.
That flock of sheep belongs to Sibyrtas of Thurii,
But to Eumaras of Sybaris, friend, these goats that you see.

LA: Did anyone ask you, by Zeus, whether the flock
Belonged to Sibyrtas or me, you oaf? How you do love to talk!

CO: Most worthy fellow, I merely state the whole truth
And boast of nothing. It's you who love to pick quarrels.

LA: Well, speak, if you've something to say, and let our friend here
Live to get back to the city. Lord, but you're long-winded,
Comatas!

CO: The Muses love me much better than Daphnis the singer,
And I sacrificed two he-goats to them a short time ago.

LA: And Apollo has great love for me, and for him

I fatten a fine ram, for the Carnea already approaches.

CO: All but two of the goats I milk have borne twins,
And the maiden, seeing me, says, "Poor lad, do you milk all alone?"

LA: Oh, fie! Lacon fills nearly twenty baskets with cheese,
And among the blossoms seduces an innocent boy.

CO: And Clearista pelts the goatherd with apples
When he passes by driving his goats, and blows him sweet kisses.

LA: And Cratidas, lithely running to meet the shepherd,
Excites me to madness; his hair shines as it brushes his neck.

CO: But neither wild rose nor anemone can be compared
With roses that grow in borders along dry-stone walls.

LA: Nor wild apples with acorns; the nuts of the oak
Have thin husks, but the apples are like golden honey.

CO: And I will shortly give the maiden a ringdove,
Taking it captive in the juniper bush where it perches.

LA: But to Cratidas I myself am going to give
A soft fleece for a cloak as soon as I shear the black ewe.

CO: Be off, you goats! Away from the wild olive tree!
Browse here on the slope of this knoll where the tamarisks grow.

LA: Get away from that oak tree, you, Conaros, Cinaitha!
Graze over there toward the east where Phalaros is.

CO: And I have a bucket of cypress wood, also a bowl,
The work of Praxiteles; these will I save for the maiden.

LA: And I have a sheep dog that tackles a wolf by the throat;
Him will I give to the lad for hunting wild beasts in the chase.

CO: You locusts who skim over the hedge of my garden,
Do not ravage my vines, for they are all withered.

LA: Cicadas, see what a spur I am to the goatherd;
Just such a spur, in truth, are you to the reapers.

CO: I hate the bushy-tailed foxes who every evening
Prowl through Micon's vineyard eating his grapes.

LA: And I hate the beetles who, borne by the wind,
Gnaw all those holes in Philondas's figs.

CO: But don't you remember that screwing I gave you, when you grinned
And wagged your tail briskly and held tight to the oak tree?

LA: I don't remember that, but I recall very well
The time Eumaras tied you up here and gave you a hiding.

CO: Already, Morson, someone is losing his temper—or didn't you notice?
Go at once and gather squills from an old woman's grave.

LA: And I, Morson, am getting somebody's goat, as you see.
Away to the Haleis and dig up cyclamen roots.

CO: May Himera flow with milk instead of water,
And may you, Crathis, redden with wine and your rushes bear fruit.

LA: And for me may Sybaris flow with honey, and at dawn
May the girl dip up with her pitcher honeycomb rather than water.

CO: My goats feed on moon-clover and succulent goatwort,
Trample herb mastic, and lie under strawberry trees.

LA: For these sheep of mine there is sweet balsam to feed on,
And rosy rock plants bloom everywhere in profusion.

CO: I have no love for Alcippa, for she did not grab me
By the ears and kiss me when lately I gave her a ringdove.

LA: But I am deeply in love with Eumedes, for when he took
The syrinx I gave him, he smothered me with his kisses.

CO: For jays to contend with nightingales, Lacon, or hoopoes with swans,
Defies law and reason, but you, poor fool, love dissension.

MORSON

I order the shepherd to stop. To you, Comatas,
Morson awards the lamb; and you, when you sacrifice
To the nymphs, send Morson promptly a choice piece of flesh.

CO: Yes, by Pan, that I will! Now bleat, all you goats
Of my herd! See what a good laugh I am going to have
On Lacon the shepherd, that I in the end
Won the lamb, and for you I will leap to the skies!
Cheer up, my horned goats! Early tomorrow morning
I'll bathe you all in Sybaris lake.
You there, you butting white billy! If you mount one of the
females
Before I've sacrificed the lamb to the nymphs,
I'll geld you! He's at it again! If I don't geld you,
May I be Melanthios instead of Comatas.

6
Pastoral Song

Damoitas and Daphnis the herdsman at one time, Aratos,
Drove their cattle to the same place. One was ruddy
With down, the beard of the other half grown. On that midday
in summer
They both sat down by a spring and sang in this fashion.
Daphnis sang first, for he had suggested the contest.

DAPHNIS

Galatea peppers your flock, Polyphemos, with apples,
And taunts you with being a man backward in love and a
goatherd,
And you, poor wretch, take no notice of her, but sit there
Playing sweet tunes on your pipe. There she is again, pelting
the dog
That watches over your sheep, and he barks
And fixes his gaze on the sea, and the lovely waves,
Gently breaking, mirror him as he runs on the shore.
Take care lest in his excitement he spring at her legs
When she comes out of the sea, and tear her fine skin.
But she flirts with you even from there; like dry thistledown
Parched by the heat of glorious summer,
She flees the lover, and when one does not love pursues,
And leaves nothing untried. For, truly, to love,
Polyphemos, oftentimes the unlovely seems lovely.

Damoitas then lifted up his voice and sang thus:

DAMOITAS

Yes, by Pan, I saw her pelting the flock.
It did not escape me—not by my one sweet eye,
With which may I see to the end (and may the prophet
Telemos, who prates of an ill to befall me,
Bear his evil home and keep it safe for his children).
But I myself, to tease her in return, don't look at her,
And tell her I have another woman, and, hearing that,
She is jealous of me, by Apollo, and mopes, and from the sea,
Nettled, keeps careful watch on my caves and my flocks.
And I goaded the dog into barking at her, for when I courted her
He would lay his snout in her lap and whimper softly.
It may be that if she sees me doing this often,
She'll send a messenger. But I'll bar the door until she swears
To spread with her own hands a fine bed for me here on the island.
And in truth my looks are not as bad as they say,
For the other day I glanced into the sea when it was calm,
And my beard looked handsome, and beautiful, too,
In my estimation, appeared my one eye, and the gleam
Of my teeth was reflected whiter than Parian marble.
But to ward off evil, I spat three times in my breast,
As the old woman Cotyttaris taught me to do.

His song having come to an end, Damoitas kissed Daphnis,
And gave him a syrinx, and Daphnis gave him a fine flute.
Damoitas played the flute, and Daphnis the herdsman the syrinx,
And the calves at once started gamboling in the soft grass.
Neither won a victory, but both were unvanquished.

7
The Harvest Festival

There once was a time when Eucritos and I, and Amyntas
Making the third, walked to the Haleis out of the city.
Phrasidamos then was making an offering of first fruits to Deo,
He and Antigenes, the two sons of Lycopeos,
Illustrious if any there be, claiming descent
From Clytia and noble Chalcon himself,
Who caused the spring Burina to bubble up underfoot
By firmly pressing against the rock with his knee;
And around it black poplars and elm trees spread out their
branches,
Weaving with their green leaves overhead an oasis of shade.
We had not yet accomplished half of our journey, nor had the
tomb
Of Brasilas come into view, when, by the grace of the Muses,
We met up with another traveler going our way—
A worthy man from Cydonia; Lycidas was his name.
He was a goatherd, and no one who saw him could doubt it,
So unmistakably did he resemble a goatherd.
Over his shoulders he wore the yellowish skin
Of a shaggy-haired goat giving off the rank smell of fresh
rennet,
And around his chest an old tunic was tightly bound
With a broad strap, and in his right hand he carried
A shepherd's crook of wild olive, and with quiet amusement
He said to me, his eyes smiling and laughter not far from his
lips,

"Simichidas, where are you off to on foot in the heat of the noon,
When even the lizard holes up in the stone wall to sleep,
And the crested larks themselves do not stir abroad?
Do you hasten as unbidden guests to a banquet, or speed to some townsman's
Winepress, that every stone sings as it spins away from your boots?"
And I answered him: "Lycidas, friend, everyone says
You are greatly distinguished among the herdsmen and reapers
For playing the syrinx; it warms my heart much to hear it,
Though, indeed, I venture to hope that I might prove your equal.
We make our way to a harvest festival; comrades of ours
Are giving a feast of first fruits of all their abundance
To honor fair-robed Demeter, for with a rich measure of barley,
Thanks to the goddess, their threshing floor overflows.
But come, since the road is common to us, and the day,
Let's have a contest of pastoral song, and perhaps each may profit.
For I too am a clear voice of the Muses,
And everyone says I am the best singer, but I'm not persuaded—
No, by heaven! To my mind, in singing I'd not yet better
Sicelidas, the noble singer from Samos, or outdo Philitas,
But vie like a frog in a singing contest with locusts."
So I spoke, with intent, and the goatherd, good-naturedly laughing,
Said, "Friend, I'll give you my staff, for you are
A scion of Zeus designed entirely for truth.
Hateful to me is the builder who tries to raise
His house as high as the peak of Oromedon mountain,
And hateful those crows of the Muses who set up their cawing

In futile contention against the minstrel from Chios.*
But come, let us at once begin the pastoral song,
Simichidas, and I— See, friend, if you like
This trifling affair I perfected of late on the mountain.

"A fair voyage to Mytilene will Ageanax have,
Though the Kids appear in the evening sky, and the south wind
Drives the wet waves, and Orion rests his foot upon Ocean,
If he save Lycidas from Aphrodite's terrible furnace,
For hot is the love of him that consumes me.
And halcyons will calm the waves and the sea and the south
wind
And the wind from the southeast that stirs the bottommost
seaweed—
Halcyons, dearest of birds to the pale sea green Nereids
And to all those whose hunting ground is the sea.
May all be propitious for Ageanax undertaking to sail
To Mytilene, and may he come safely to harbor after his
voyage.
And I on that day, wearing a wreath on my head made of dill
Or roses or stock, shall drink from the bowl the Ptelean wine
And recline by the fire, and someone shall roast for me beans on
the coals.
And my pallet of straw shall be strewn to the depth of my
elbow
With fleabane and asphodel mingled with curly green parsley.
And, drinking at ease, I shall remember Ageanax
In the very cups, and press my lip to the lees.
And two shepherds shall play to me on the flute, one from
Acharnae,
One from Lycope, and Tityros, standing nearby, shall sing

* Homer.

Of how once on a time Daphnis the herdsman yearned for
Xenea,
And how the mountain grieved and the oak trees lamented
That grew along the banks of the river Himera
When he was wasting like snow on the slopes of high Haimos
Or Athos or Rhodope or the far distant Caucasus.
And he shall sing of how once, by the cruel command of his
lord,
The wide coffer swallowed the goatherd while he was yet living,
And how the blunt-nosed bees, lured by the fragrance of cedar,
Flew out of the meadow and fed him with delicate flowers,
Because the Muse had poured on his lips her sweet nectar.
O blessed Comatas, yours was this pleasant affliction;
You too were shut up in a coffer and fed by the bees
On honeycomb, and endured that fate for a year.
Would that among the living of my time you had been counted,
So that I could have tended your goats for you on the mountain,
Hearing the sound of your voice as you, godlike Comatas,
Lay under the oaks and the fir trees and sang your sweet songs."

So much he sang and came to an end, and I, in return,
Spoke in this way: "Lycidas, friend, while on the mountain
Grazing my herd, many a song have the nymphs also taught
me—
Good songs whose fame may have reached even Zeus on his
throne.
But this greatly surpasses them all, and with this I begin
In your honor. Listen, then, for you are dear to the Muses.

"The Loves sneezed on Simichidas, truly, for he,
Poor fellow, loves Myrto as goats love the spring.
But Aratos, the dearest friend a man ever had,
Yearns deep in his heart for a boy. Aristis knows—

That noble man, the best of them all, whom Phoebus himself
Would not disdain to have sing with the phorminx* alongside
his tripods—
How Aratos burns to the marrow for love of a boy.
O Pan, who have for your lot the lovely plain of Homole,
Let the youth lie unbidden within his dear arms,
Whether he be the dainty Philinos or whether another.
If such is your will, O dear Pan, then may the Arcadian boys
Nevermore whip you about your ribs and your shoulders
With squills whenever they suffer a shortage of meat.
But if you will not, then may you be bitten all over
And scratch head to foot with your nails, and bed down on
nettles;
And in midwinter may you be in the Edonian mountains,
Turned toward the river Hebros up by the North Pole,
And in summer among the farthest Ethiopians pasture your
flock
Under the Blemyan rock out of sight of the Nile.
But you, Loves, leave the sweet springs of Hyetis and Byblis,
And Oecos, the lofty abode of golden Dione—
O Loves, rosy as apples—
And shoot with your bows for me at charming Philinos;
Shoot him, for the villain shows my comrade no mercy.
And riper, indeed, is he than a pear, and the women
Exclaim, 'Alas, Philinos, your lovely bloom falls away!'
Let us no longer keep watch at his doorstep, Aratos,
Or wear out our feet, but let the cock crowing at daybreak
Deliver another to the pain and the numbness.
Hereafter, friend, let Molon alone be choked in that wrestling
arena.

* A form of lyre or harp.

Let our care be tranquillity, and may a crone,
Spitting, ward off from us the unlovely."

So much my song, and Lycidas, as before sweetly laughing,
Gave me his staff as a parting gift of the Muses,
And then, veering left, took the road leading to Pyxa.
But Eucritos and I and pretty Amyntas
Turned toward Phrasidamos' farm, and there we lay down
rejoicing
On deep beds of sweet-smelling rushes and freshly stripped vine
leaves.
Overhead rustled many black poplars and elm trees,
And sacred water chuckled and gurgled nearby
As it trickled forth from the cave of the nymphs.
Dusky locusts were hard at their chirping on shady branches,
And from afar the tree frog crooned in the dense thornbush,
And the crested larks and the linnets sang, the turtledove
mourned,
And the yellow bees buzzed as they hovered around the clear
spring.
All was fragrant with the rich summer, the odors of fruit time.
Pears by our feet, by our sides apples
In lavish abundance were rolling, and the boughs
Of the plum trees, heavy laden, drooped to the ground.
And the four-year seal was loosed from the head of the wine
jars.
Nymphs of Castalia who haunt the peak of Parnassos,
Could it have been such a bowl that old Cheiron offered
To Heracles in the rocky cavern of Pholos?
Was it such nectar that set the feet of the shepherd
(Mighty Polyphemos, who pelted ships with whole mountains)
To dancing among his sheepfolds by the Anapos?—

Such nectar as on that day you mixed for us, nymphs,
At the altar by the threshing floor of Demeter? On her mound
May I once again plant the great winnowing fan, while she
Stands by smiling, holding in both hands sheaves and poppies.

8

(Second Pastoral Song)

DAPHNIS AND MENALCAS

Menalcas, they say, while on the high mountain tending his flock,
Met up with the charming Daphnis grazing his cattle.
Both were red-headed, both not yet fully grown,
Both had learned to play on the syrinx, both of them sang.
Seeing Daphnis, Menalcas spoke to him first.
"Daphnis, guardian of lowing cows, will you sing with me?
If I sing as long as I want to, I say I'll beat you."
And Daphnis then answered him in these words:
"Shepherd of woolly sheep, pipe-playing Menalcas,
Never will you beat me, not if you hurt yourself singing."

MENALCAS

Are you game to find out? Are you willing to put up a bet?

DAPHNIS

I'm game to find out; I'm willing to put up a bet.

ME: And now what shall we settle on as a suitable stake?
DA: I'll stake a bull calf, and you stake that lamb as big as its mother.
ME: Never will I bet a lamb, for my father is hard,
And my mother, and they count all the sheep every evening.
DA: Then what will you bet? What reward will there be for the victor?
ME: I have a syrinx I made, a lovely one with nine notes,
With white beeswax evenly spread below and above.
That will I bet, but not what belongs to my father.
DA: Truly, I too have a syrinx having nine notes,

With white beeswax evenly spread below and above.
Only lately I put it together, and this finger still hurts
Where the reed I was working with split and cut me.

ME: But who will judge us? Who will give us a hearing?

DA: That goatherd yonder—look. Let's call him over.
The one around whose kids the dog with the white patch is barking.

So the boys shouted, and the goatherd came at their call,
And the boys were ready to sing and the goatherd willing to judge them.
First clear-voiced Menalcas sang, the lot having fallen to him,
Then Daphnis took up the answering strain of pastoral song.
And Menalcas, beginning first, sang in this way:

ME: Valleys and rivers, race of the gods, if ever
Menalcas the piper has pleased you with a song,
With all your soul feed his ewe lambs, and if by chance
Daphnis comes with his calves, no less may he have.

DA: Springs and pastures, sweet herbage, if indeed Daphnis
Rivals the nightingales themselves with his singing,
Fatten this herd of cattle, and if Menalcas
Drives his flock here, welcome him and let him feed all in abundance.

ME: There sheep, there goats bear twins, there bees swarm
Filling the hive, and oak trees grow taller
Where the fair Milon sets foot, but when he leaves,
Parched is the shepherd there and parched are the pastures.

DA: Everywhere spring, everywhere pastures, everywhere milk
Gushes forth from the udders, and the newborn calves thrive
Where the fair Naïs wanders, but when she departs,
Withered is the herdsman and withered his cattle.

ME: O goat, mate of white she-goats, to the unfathomed depth of the
woodland—
Here, you flat-nosed kids, here to the water!—
For he is there. Go, shorthorn, and say, "Milon,
Proteus herded seals though he was a god."

. . . *

ME: Not for me the land of Pelops, nor would I have
The talents of Croesus, or outrun the winds;
But under this rock would I sing, holding you in my arms
And gazing out at our pasturing flocks and the Sicilian sea.

DA: A dread affliction is winter to trees, to waters a drought,
To birds the snare, and to wild game the net;
But to man the desire for an innocent maiden. O father Zeus,
Not alone am I lovesick, for you too lust after women.

Thus the boys sang, each taking his turn in alternate stanzas;
Then Menalcas led off the concluding round of the contest.

ME: Wolf, stay away from my kids, stay away from their dams,
And do me no harm that though small I watch over so many.
Lampuros, dog of mine, are you so sound asleep?
Deep sleep is not right when you herd the flock with a boy.
Sheep, don't be shy of eating your fill of the tender young grass;
Before you begin to tire, it will grow back again.
Go to it! Feed, feed, and fill all your udders,
So the lambs may have their share and I too have some for
my cheese trays.

Secondly, Daphnis raised up his song in clear, ringing tones.

DA: Yesterday from her cave a girl with joining brows saw me
As I drove my calves past, and said I was lovely, lovely.

* A stanza attributed to Daphnis is missing.

But not even with a bitter remark did I answer,
But with my eyes cast down went on my way.
Sweet the voice of the heifer, sweet too her breath,
And sweet in summer to lie out of doors beside running water.
To the oak tree acorns belong, to the apple tree apples,
To the cow the calf, to the herdsman his cattle alone.

So sang the boys, and so at length spoke the goatherd:
"Sweet are your lips, O Daphnis, and lovely your voice.
Better is it to hear you sing than to lick honey.
Take the syrinxes, for you are the victor in singing.
But if you will teach me to sing myself as I pasture my goats,
I will give you as a fee for the lessons that hornless she-goat
Who always fills the milk pail till it brims over."
As the boy, exultant over his triumph, cavorted, clapping his hands,
So might a fawn playfully bound near its mother.
And as the other, grief-stricken, smoldered at heart,
So might an unhappy bride grieve over her marriage.
From that day Daphnis ranked first among the herdsmen,
And while still only a youth married Naïs the nymph.

9

(Third Pastoral Song)

DAPHNIS AND MENALCAS

Sing a pastoral song, Daphnis. You begin the song first—
Begin the song, Daphnis, and let Menalcas then follow,
When you have put the calves to the cows and the bulls to the
heifers.
Let them graze with the herd and wander about in the leaves,
But not stray away, while you sing me a pastoral song
From your side and Menalcas in turn sings back from the other.

DAPHNIS

Sweet is the call of the calf, and sweet the cow's lowing,
Sweet sound the syrinx and herdsman, and sweet too sound I.
I have a bed beside the cold water, and on it are piled
Fine hides from my white heifers—all tossed off the cliff
By the southwester as they browsed on arbutus.
I care as much for the roasting heat of the summer
As a lover for his father's advice and his mother's.

So did Daphnis sing to me, and thus sang Menalcas:

MENALCAS

My mother is Etna, and in a fine cave in the hollow rocks
Do I live, and my wealth is all one could dream of.
Many a ewe have I, and many a she-goat,
And their fleeces lie at my head and my feet.
Sausages boil and acorns roast on an oakwood fire

When the weather is stormy, and no more care I for the winter
Than a toothless man for nuts when cake is at hand.

I clapped my hands for them both and gave each one a gift:
To Daphnis a staff from my father's farm in the country—
In its natural shape, but not even a craftsman would fault it—
And to Menalcas a beautiful shell I myself had taken
Among the Icarian rocks and had fed on, dividing the flesh
In five portions, we being five; and he blew a blast on his shell.

Hail to you, pastoral Muses, and make known the song
I myself sang at the time I met with those herdsmen:
And may pimples no longer grow on the tip of my tongue.*

Cicada is dear to cicada, red ant to red ant,
Falcon to falcon, but the Muses and sweet song to me;
May their presence fill my whole house. For sleep is not
sweeter,
Nor the sudden coming of spring, nor flowers to bees,
So dear to me are the Muses. For those whom they look upon
With delight the drugged potions of Circe can never destroy.

* A penalty for the misuse of speech, either by speaking falsely or by withholding the truth.

10

Farmer and Reapers

MILON

Bucaios, you property owner, what is the matter, poor fellow?
You can't even cut a straight swath today as you used to,
Or keep abreast of your neighbor in reaping, but lag behind
Like a sheep of the flock whose foot has been pricked by a
cactus.
What will you be like by midday, much less by evening,
If at the beginning you cannot bite into your furrow?

BUCAIOS

Milon, you glutton for reaping, you chip of the unyielding rock,
Have you never happened to long for someone who's absent?

MI: Never. What longing has a laborer except for his labor?
BU: Have you never happened to lie awake all night for love?
MI: No, may that not be. It's bad for a dog to taste leather.
BU: But I, Milon, have been in love for nearly ten days.
MI: Clearly you tap the wine jar; vinegar is my drink and little of
that.
BU: And so everything outside my door has gone without hoeing
since seedtime.
MI: Which charmer so possesses you?
BU: Polybotas' girl,
Who the other day at Hippocion's played the flute for the
reapers.
MI: God finds the sinner! You've got what you have long wished
for—
A praying mantis to snuggle up to at night.

BU: You're starting to taunt me! Plutos alone is not blind;
Dunderheaded Eros is also, so stop talking big.

MI: I'm not talking big. You just mow down the crop
And strike up a love song to the girl. Happier so
Will you work—and you were at one time a singer.

BU: Pierian Muses, join with me in a song about the slim maiden,
For, goddesses, all that you touch you make lovely.
Charming Bombyca, everyone calls you the Syrian,
Skinny and sun scorched; but honey golden do I alone say you are.
Dark is the violet too, and the hyacinth with its letters,
Yet in garlands they come first of all, as everyone knows.
The goat pursues clover, the wolf the plump goat,
The crane the plow, but I for you am demented.
O that I had as much as Croesus was said once to own!
To Aphrodite I would dedicate golden statues of both—
You with your flute in your hand and a rose or an apple,
I in new clothing and shod in new shoes of Amyclae.
Lovely Bombyca, like knucklebones are your feet,
Your voice like syrup, but no word do I know for your ways.

MI: We had not been aware that Buco composed a good song;
How skillfully he measured his lines and gave shape to his fancy!
Shame on my beard, which I seem to have grown to no purpose.
But listen to this one by the divine Lityerses.

Demeter, rich in fruit and in grain, grant that this crop
Be harvested well and be abundantly fruitful.
Bind up the sheaves, you binders, lest a passerby say,

"These men are good for nothing; here are more wages
wasted."
See that the cut end of your swath be toward the north wind
Or toward the west; richer so will the ears be.
When you are threshing the crop, shun sleep at noon,
For then the grain most readily parts from the stalk.
When you reap, start work when the crested lark first awakes
And stop when it seeks slumber, but rest out the heat.
O for the life of a frog, boys! No care has he
For one to pour out his drink; it is around him in plenty.
Overseer, boil the lentils better, you miser,
Lest you cut your hand with all this cumin-seed splitting.

That's the kind of song for men who work in the sun,
Bucaios; your famished love is fit for telling
Your mother as she wakes up in bed in the morning.

11

Cyclops

No other medicine is a specific for love,
Nicias, nor salve, it seems to me, nor yet poultice,
But the Pierian Muses. Light is this cure for mankind,
Even sweet, though to find it is not ever easy.
But you know this well, I suppose, being a doctor
And better beloved than most by the nine Muses.
So at least most easily fared my neighbor the Cyclops,
Polyphemos of old, when he loved Galatea,
Just at the time his beard was sprouting about his mouth and his
temples.
But he loved her not with apples or roses or ringlets
But with downright madness, holding all else incidental.
Often his sheep would come back to the fold by themselves
From the green pasture, while he himself, singing to Galatea
From break of day, pined away all alone on the shore strewn
with seaweed,
Bearing under his heart a festering wound,
His vitals having been pierced by the shaft of great Cypris.
But he found the medicine; sitting on a high cliff
Looking out over the sea, he sang in this way:

O white Galatea, why do you spurn your lover,
Whiter than curd cheese to look at, softer than the lamb,
More skittery than the calf, smoother than the green grape?
Why do you come here whenever sweet sleep has claimed me,
But hurry away as soon as sweet sleep lets me go,

Fleeing just like a sheep who sees the gray wolf?
I have loved you, darling, ever since you first came
With my mother,* wishing to pick hyacinth blossoms
Up on the mountain, and I led the way.
And from that day I first saw you right up to now
I cannot stop—but you don't care; no, by Zeus, not at all.
I know, darling girl, the reason why you avoid me—
Because of the shaggy eyebrow across my whole forehead
That stretches in one long line from one ear to the other
With one eye underneath, and the flat nose over my lips.
But such as I am, I pasture a thousand fine sheep
And squeeze from them and drink the very best milk.
Nor am I lacking for cheese, either in summer or autumn
Or at the height of winter; my cheese baskets always run over.
I know how to pipe like none of the other Cyclopes here,
And often I sing of you late at night, my sweet honey apple,
And of myself. Eleven fawns I am raising for you,
All wearing collars, and also four bear cubs.
But come here to me; I promise you won't be worse off.
Leave the green sea to surge in and out on the shore.
Your nights will be sweeter spent in the cave beside me.
Here there are laurels, here slender cypresses,
Here black ivy, here a vine with sweet fruit,
Here cold water provided by tree-laden Etna
From white snow freshly fallen—a drink for immortals.
Who would choose the sea and its waves over these?
But if I myself appear too shaggy for you,
I have oak logs and under the ashes an undying fire;
I offer you my very soul to burn, too,
And my one eye—and there is nothing more precious to me.
Alas that my mother did not give me gills at my birth,

* The sea nymph Thoösa; his father was Poseidon.

So I could sink down to you and at least kiss your hand
If your lips are unwilling. I would bring you white snowdrops,
Or delicate poppies, red, and having broad petals;
But poppies bloom in the summer, snowdrops in winter,
So I could not offer you all these gifts at one time.
But now, little darling, right now I will learn how to swim,
If to this island some stranger should sail in a ship,
So I will know why you all delight to live in the deep.
Oh, please come out, Galatea, and then please forget,
Just as I do now, sitting here, to go home again.
Come pasture the sheep with me and help with the milking
And set the cheese by putting in the sharp rennet.
My mother alone does me wrong, and I hold her to blame,
That never a kindly word does she speak to you about me,
Though she sees me on your account growing thin day by day.
I will tell her how my head aches and both my feet throb,
So she may suffer as I myself also suffer.
O Cyclops, Cyclops, where have your wits flown to?
If you would go and weave baskets, and for your lambs
Gather fresh shoots, you would quickly come to your senses.
Milk the ewe that is here; why chase the one fleeing?
Maybe you'll find another and even more fair Galatea.
Many a girl invites me to be her playmate at nighttime,
And they all giggle coyly whenever I take any notice.
It's clear that on land even I appear to be someone.

So Polyphemos assuaged his love with a song,
And came through the ordeal much better than if he'd paid
gold.

12

The Favorite

You have come, darling boy! At last after two nights and days
You have come! But those anxious with longing grow old in a day.
As much sweeter spring is than winter, as apple than beach plum,
As thicker the wool of the sheep than that of her lamb,
As a maiden is more to be prized than a thrice-married woman,
As more nimble is a fawn than a calf, and the nightingale's song
Clearer than that of all other winged creatures,
So great is my joy at your coming, and to you I run
Like a wayfarer parched by the sun to the shade of the oak.
O that the Loves might breathe alike on us both,
That we two might become a legend for all men hereafter!
"Divine were they among those who lived in earlier times,
The one the inspirer," as a man of Amyclae might put it,
"The other the mirror," as a Thessalian might say,
"And under an equal yoke did they love one another.
Then were there golden men, when the beloved reflected the love of the lover."
O father Zeus and you ageless immortals, if it might be!
If after two hundred or more generations have passed,
Someone might bring me a message in Acheron, whence none return:
"The love between you and your devoted companion is still
On the lips of all men, but young men most of all."

But this, to be sure, rests with the heavenly powers;
It will be as they ordain. When I sing in praise of your charms,
Over my narrow nose I shall raise no pimples for lying,
For if sometimes you sting me as well, you at once make amends
And doubly delight me, and at parting my measure runs over.
Men of Megarian Nisaea, skilled with the oar,
May your lives prosper, for beyond others you honored
Your Attic guest, Diocles, who gave his life for his love.
Around his tomb ever at the beginning of springtime
Crowds of boys gather and vie for the kissing award,
And he who more sweetly presses lip against lip
Goes home to his mother proudly laden with garlands.
Happy is he who judges those kisses of boys!
Truly, many a prayer must he offer to bright-eyed Ganymedes
To have a mouth like the Lydian stone,* by which money-
changers
Cannily separate counterfeit coin from true gold.

* A mineral used as a touchstone found on Mt. Tmolus in Lydia in central Asia Minor.

13
Hylas

Not for us only, Nicias, as we imagined,
Was Eros born to whoever of the gods it was who begot him,
Nor are we the first to whom the lovely seems lovely,
Mortals knowing nothing of what comes tomorrow.
For even Amphitryon's son,* the bronze-hearted hero
Who stood fast against the fierce lion, once loved a lad,
Little Hylas, a winsome curly-haired child,
And taught him, as a father would his dear son,
All he knew that had made him a good man and famous.
He was never apart from him, either when noon came upon
them,
Or when Dawn with her white horses drove up to the palace of
Zeus,
Or when chickens, sleepily cheeping, looked to their roost
When their mother shook out her wings on the smoke-blackened
perch,
That the boy might be molded in his own likeness
And under his guidance grow up to the ideal of manhood.
So when Jason, the son of Aison, sailed off to recover
The golden fleece, and with him went all the noblest men
From the cities, chosen heroes famed for their exploits,
Then also to wealthy Iolcos went the man much-enduring,
The son of Alcmene,* royal queen of Midea,

* Heracles: his mother was Alcmene, his father Amphitryon or, according to legend, Zeus.

And with Hylas beside him went down to the stoutly benched
Argo,
A ship that never touched the blue clashing rocks
But sprang forth between them and over the great sea flew like
an eagle
To the deep Phasis; and the rocks thereafter stood anchored.
But when the Pleiades rise, and the outlying hills
Pasture the new lambs, spring already yielding to summer,
That godlike band of picked heroes gave thought to sailing,
And settled down in their places within the hollow ship *Argo*,
And with a south wind blowing, reached the Hellespont on the
third day,
And put in to harbor in the Propontis, where the oxen
Of the Cianians cleave broad furrows with the bright plowshare.
At evening they disembarked on the beach, and prepared their
meal
Two by two, but spread out one bed for them all,
For nearby was a meadow with growing things in abundance
For bedding, where they cut sharp sedge and tall galingale.
Golden-haired Hylas scampered off with a brass pitcher
To fetch water for Heracles' and loyal Telamon's supper,
For both comrades always sat down to dine at one table.
In a short time the boy saw a spring
In a low-lying place; rushes grew thickly around it
And celandine and feathery maidenhair fern
And lush green parsley and marsh-loving mule-grass.
But at mid-depth in the water nymphs were arranging their
dance,
Unsleeping nymphs, dread goddesses to folk who live in the
country,
Eunicë, Malis, and Nychea with spring in her eyes.
Eagerly the lad leaned down to dip his capacious brass pitcher
Into the spring, but all of them clung to his hand,

For love of the Argive boy had flurried each tender heart,
And he plunged headlong into the black water,
As when a flaming star suddenly falls out of heaven
Into the sea, and a sailor says to his comrades,
"Lighten the rigging, boys; a fair wind for sailing!"
While the nymphs, holding the weeping boy in their laps,
Sought to comfort him with gentle endearments,
The son of Amphitryon, troubled by the boy's absence,
Went off in pursuit, taking his double-curved Scythian bow
And his club, which he ever carried in his right hand.
Three times he shouted "Hylas!" as loud as his deep throat
could bellow,
And three times the boy answered, but his voice came faintly
From under the water, sounding far off though very nearby.
As when the noble lion who feeds on raw flesh,
Hearing afar a fawn crying in the mountains,
Hastens from its lair toward the ready-made feast,
So Heracles, yearning after the boy,
Raged through the untrodden thorns and ranged far and wide.
Unflinching are lovers, and unremitting his toil
As he scoured hills and oak groves, and all Jason's affair was
forgotten.
The ship was ready to sail and the men were aboard,
But at midnight the godlike heroes again lowered the sail,
Waiting for Heracles; but he stormed dementedly on
Where his feet led, for within him the cruel god tore at his
heart.
Thus is lovely Hylas numbered among the immortals.
But the heroes derided Heracles for abandoning ship
And deserting his comrades aboard the thirty-benched *Argo*,
And he went on foot to the Colchians and the unwelcoming
Phasis.

14

Aischinas and Thyonichos

AISCHINAS
Very glad to see you, Thyonichos, man.
THYONICHOS
Same here, Aischinas.
It's been a long time.
AI: A long time indeed.
TH: How goes it with you?
AI: Not very well, Thyonichos.
TH: That's why you're so thin, then,
And why your mustache is so long and your curls in a tangle.
The other day a Pythagorean arrived looking the same,
Sallow and barefoot; he said he was an Athenian.
AI: Was he in love too?
TH: Yes, with wheat loaves, to my thinking.
AI: Have your joke, friend. But the lovely Cynisca has scorned me.
One of these days I expect I'll go mad; I'm a hair from it now.
TH: That's always your way, dear Aischinas—inclined to be hasty,
And wanting everything just to your liking. But tell me the latest.
AI: A man from Argos and I and a Thessalian horseman named Agis
And a soldier, Cleunicos, were having a drinking party
At my place in the country. I had killed two chickens for them
And a suckling pig, and opened up the Bibline wine,
As fragrant after four years, almost, as when it was pressed;
And I set out some scallions and snails. It was a fine party!

After a while we had a notion to toast
Each one his dearest, but the favorite had to be named.
We all named our toast as we drank, as we had agreed,
But Cynisca, though I was right there, said nothing. Think how
    I felt!
"Nothing to say for yourself?" someone said, teasing. "Do you
    see a wolf?"*
"How clever!" she answered, and blushed—her cheeks would
    have lighted a lamp.
A Wolf is there indeed—Lycos, the son of Labes, my neighbor,
Tall, smooth, good-looking in the opinion of many.
It was for him that she burned with that well-known grand
    passion.
A hint of it had come to my ears a short time before,
But I paid no attention: what good is a beard to a man?
The four of us were already deep in our cups,
And the one from Larissa maliciously started to sing
A Thessalian song, "My Lycos," from the beginning,
And Cynisca suddenly started to cry, more bitterly
Than a six-year-old girl vainly cries for the lap of her mother.
Then—you know how I am, Thyonichos—I gave her a sock in
    the face
With my fist, then hit her again, and she caught up her skirts
And ran rapidly out. "You slut!" I yelled. "So I'm not good
    enough for you!
Someone else is sweeter to cuddle? Go warm up your other
    darling!
For him are your tears? Let them flow bigger than apples!"
The swallow who brings a tidbit to her nestlings under the eaves
Flies swiftly off again to gather more food;
Even more swiftly did Cynisca fly from her cushions

* There is a pun here on "Lycos," which means "wolf" in Greek.

Straight out through the foyer and the front door as her feet led her.
As the fable goes, "The bull once went to the forest."
Twenty, add eight, add nine, add ten again.
Today's the eleventh. In two days it's a good two months*
We've been away from each other. If I were shorn Thracian-wise,
She wouldn't know. Now Lycos is all, and to Lycos her door is open at night,
And I am altogether out of the reckoning—
Like the wretched Megarians, trailing the list.
If I could fall out of love, I could keep going.
But now what? The mouse, as they say, Thyonichos, has tangled with pitch,
And what drug there may be for hopeless passion
I do not know. Though Simos, who fell for that bronze-plated charmer,
Shipped abroad and returned sane and sound—a man of my age.
And I too will sail overseas. A soldier's life
Is neither the worst nor the best, but better than average.

TH: I wish things had worked out to your heart's liking, Aischinas.
But if you're really thinking of leaving the country,
Ptolemy is the best paymaster for a free man.

AI: What kind of man is he otherwise?

TH: The very best.
Considerate, cultured, courtly, exceedingly pleasant;
Knows the worth of a friend, and a foe even better;
Gives lavishly, as a king should, and doesn't refuse
If he's asked. But a fellow shouldn't always be asking, Aischinas.

* Calendars varied from city to city, but the calculation is apparently based on a thirty-day month.

So if you have a mind to buckle your mantle
On your right shoulder, and can stand firm on both feet
To meet the assault of a resolute warrior,
Off to Egypt at once. We're all going gray
At the temple, and time creeps down the jaw,
Frosting hair after hair. One must act while the knee is still
limber.

15

The Adonis Festival

GORGO AND PRAXINOË

GORGO

Is Praxinoë in?

PRAXINOË

Dear Gorgo! It's been so long! Yes, I'm at home.
How wonderful that at last you have come! Eunoë, see to a chair for her,
And find her a cushion.

GO: No, this is just fine.

PR: Do sit down.

GO: Oh, I'm so flustered! I barely escaped with my life,
Praxinoë. Such a huge crowd! So many chariots,
Men in boots, men wearing short cloaks, all over the place!
And the road is endless. You live farther and farther away.

PR: It's that husband of mine! He comes to the ends of the earth
And takes not a house but a hut to keep neighbors apart,
Just out of spite, the jealous fool—he's always the same.

GO: Dear, you shouldn't talk that way about Dinon, your husband,
In front of the little one. See how he looks at you, woman!
It's all right, Zopyrion, sweetie. She doesn't mean daddy.

PR: By all that's holy, the sprat understands!

GO: Daddy's nice!

PR: That daddy the other day—the other day I said to him,
"Papa, get some red dye and soda when you go to the market,"
And he came back bringing me salt—a man twelve feet high!

GO: Mine's the same way. Diocleides has absolutely no sense about
money.
Yesterday he paid seven drachmas for dog's hair,
Shreds of old purses—five fleeces, all filthy—work upon work.
But come, change your dress and put on your mantle.
We're going to our rich King Ptolemy's palace
To see the Adonis. The queen, I hear, has arranged
A magnificent show.

PR: To the blessed, all is a blessing.

GO: You can talk about what you've seen when you've seen it and
someone else hasn't.
It's time to be going.

PR: It's always a holiday for the idle.
Eunoë, pick up that yarn. Leave it lying about again
And I'll scalp you. Cats like a soft bed to lie in.
Hurry up. Bring water quickly. One needs water first,
So she brings the soap. Never mind, let me have it. Not so
much, wastrel!
Pour the water. Must you splash my chiton,* you moron?
Stop, that's enough! There, I have washed as well as the gods
will allow.
Where's the key of the big chest? Bring it here.

GO: Praxinoë, that full-draped fashion vastly becomes you.
Is it too much to ask how much it cost off the loom?

PR: Don't remind me, Gorgo! More than a mina or two
Of good silver. And I put my soul in the handwork as well.

GO: But it turned out wonderfully well—you've got to say that.

PR: Now bring my cloak and my sun hat. Drape it around me
So it hangs right. No, child, you can't come. Gr-r-r! Horsey
bites!
Cry all you like. It won't do for you to be lamed.

* The basic Greek garment, of varying length, worn by both men and women.

Let's be on our way. Phrygia, take care of the mite and amuse him.
Call the dog inside and lock the house door.

Ye gods, what a crowd! How and when will we ever
Get through this mob? Ants without number or measure!
You've done many commendable things, Ptolemy,
Since your father has been among the immortals. No villain
Creeps up upon one in the street, Egyptian-wise, bent on mischief,
As in the past—a trick that pack of rogues used to play,
One as bad as the other, all of them scoundrels.
Dearest Gorgo! What will become of us now?
The king's horse troops! My dear man, don't trample on me!
The chestnut's reared straight up! How wild he is! Stand back,
Eunoë! Don't be so reckless! He'll kill the man holding the bridle!
How thankful I am that baby's safely at home!

GO: Never mind, Praxinoë. Now they've left us behind,
And gone on their way.

PR: And already I'm almost myself.
A horse and a cold snake have filled me with terror
Since I was a child. Let's hurry. The crowd is pouring upon us.

GO: From the palace, mother?

OLD WOMAN

Yes, dearie.

GO: Then it's not hard
To get in?

OLD WOMAN

By trying, the Achaians got into Troy,
Pretty children. By trying, everything can be accomplished.

GO: The old lady utters her oracle and goes on her way.

PR: Women know everything, even how Zeus married Hera.

GO: Look at that crowd around the doors, Praxinoë!

PR: Horrors! Gorgo, give me your hand. And, Eunoë,
Hold on tight to Eutychis' hand so you won't go astray.
Let's all go in together. Stay close behind us, Eunoë.
Oh, I could cry! My summer wrap is already ripped
In two, Gorgo! For heaven's sake, sir, as you hope
For happiness, please have some regard for my mantle.

STRANGER
It wasn't my fault, but I'll try to watch out.

PR: What a crowd, truly!
They jostle like pigs.

STRANGER
Cheer up, ladies, now we're all right.

PR: And may *you* be all right forever and ever, dear man,
For looking after us. What a kind, considerate fellow!
Eunoë's hemmed in—poor lamb, push your way through!
Good! "All inside," as the bridegroom said, shutting the door.

GO: Praxinoë, come here and look at these tapestries first!
How finely woven and charming! Fit for robes for the gods, one would say!

PR: Lady Athene, what weavers they must have been—
What artists to have made the figures so lifelike!
How naturally they stand and seem to be moving,
As if they were living, not woven. What a clever thing man is!
And this! What a wonder! See how he reclines on his silver couch,
With the first silky down creeping over his cheeks!
Adonis thrice-loved, in Acheron, even, held dear.

ANOTHER STRANGER
Stop it, you tiresome women! An end to your chatter,

You cooing doves. They wear you out with that everlasting
broad accent.

PR: Holy mother! Where does this fellow come from? What's it to
you how we talk?
Give orders to those beneath you. It's Syracusans you speak to.
And, so you may know, we're Corinthians by descent,
As Bellerophon was. It's Peloponnesian we speak;
And Dorians, it seems to me, are allowed to speak Doric.
Let there be no masters above us, Melita, but one.
Your opinion is nothing to me. Don't waste your breath.

GO: Hush, Praxinoë. The Argive woman's daughter is ready to sing
The hymn to Adonis—a most erudite musician—
The one whose dirge last year was considered the best.
Her performance I know will be lovely. She's already clearing
her throat.

SINGER

Mistress, you who love Golgoi and Idalion
And lofty Eryx, Aphrodite with playthings of gold,
Now out of eternal Acheron the soft-footed Hours
Have led Adonis back to you in the twelfth month,*
The dear Hours, slowest of the blessed, whose coming
Is longed for, ever bearing a boon to all mortals.
Cypris, daughter of Dione, you, as men say,
Made mortal Berenicë immortal,
Dropping ambrosia into her womanly breast.
And to honor you, goddess of many names, many shrines,
Berenicë's daughter, Arsinoë, lovely as Helen,
Showers on Adonis all beautiful things.
Beside him lie the fruits the trees bring forth in their season,

* The festival is an annual event, apparently in late summer. My guess is that the year began with the flooding of the Nile in the fall.

Beside him delicate cresses tended in baskets of silver,
And golden flacons of Syrian myrrh,
And as many cakes as the women concoct on their cake boards,
Intermixing colorful blossoms with the white flour,
Those blended with honey and those with glistening oil;
And every creature is here that flies or treads on the earth.
Green bowers redolent of feathery dill
Have been raised, and youthful Loves flutter above them
Like fledgling nightingales that make trial of their wings,
Flitting from bough to bough on a tree.
O ebony! O gold! O eagles carved of white ivory
That carry to Zeus son of Cronos a lad to pour out his wine,*
And the purple coverlets on it softer than sleep!
Miletos will say, as will the shepherd of Samos,
"To us was it given to spread the couch for lovely Adonis."
Cypris is holding him, and rosy-armed Adonis holds her.
The bridegroom is eighteen or nineteen years old;
His kiss does not wound, for the golden down is still on his lip.
Farewell now to Cypris holding her man in her arms.
But at dawn, in the dew, we will all gather together
And carry him out to where the waves splash on the shore,
Loosing our hair and letting our garments fall to our ankles,
And with bared breasts begin the clear-ringing song.
O dear Adonis, both earth and Acheron do you frequent,
Unique, as they tell us, among demigods. Agamemnon
Knew no such fate, nor mighty Ajax, wrath-consumed hero,
Nor Hector, eldest son of Hecuba, mother of twenty.
Nor Patroclos, nor Pyrrhos returning from Troy,
Nor the Lapiths of earlier times and Deucalion's seed,

* Ganymedes; the passage describes the elaborate frame of the couch on which the figures of Aphrodite and Adonis are lying.

Nor Pelops' line and the Pelasgian chieftains of Argos.
Bless us next year as well, dear Adonis. Joyful are we
At your coming now, and joyful will be your return.

GO: Praxinoë, how very accomplished that woman is—
Happy in knowing so much, happier still in so sweet a voice!
Well, it's time to go home. Diocleides hasn't had dinner.
The man's sour enough, but when he's hungry don't even go near him!
Farewell, Adon, beloved, and welcome when you come back!

16
The Graces

Ever is it a care to the daughters of Zeus, ever to minstrels,
To hymn the immortals, to hymn the glory of heroes.
The Muses are goddesses, and goddesses sing of the gods,
But we are mortals here, and as mortals let us celebrate mortals.
Who of all who live beneath the bright light of day
Will open his house to give our Graces glad welcome
And not send them away again empty-handed?
Barefoot and angry, they come trudging back home
And jeer at me much for the vain road they have traveled,
And huddle down again on the floor of an empty chest
Disconsolate, letting their heads fall to their cold knees—
Their resting place always when they have returned
unsuccessful.
Who is there now? Who will entertain one who speaks with fair
words?
I do not know; for men no longer aspire to win praise
For noble deeds, as in former ages, but look to advantage.
All keep their hands in their pockets, alert for ways
To get money, and to no one give even the tarnish they rub off a
coin,
But are quick to say, "The shank is farther away than the knee;
Misfortune may come to me." "The gods reward minstrels."
"Who wants to hear another one? Homer is sufficient for all."
"The best bard is the one who takes nothing from me."

Poor fools, what good are vast hoards of gold lying inside your coffers?
This is not to thoughtful men the advantage of wealth,
But to nourish the soul, and perhaps give some to a singer;
To benefit many a kinsman, and many other men too,
Always to sacrifice to the gods at their altars,
Not to act the churlish host, but to treat guests kindly
At your table and send them on their way when they wish to be gone,
But especially to honor the sacred priests of the Muses,
So that even when hidden in Hades' realm you will be heard of,
And not weep without fame upon bleak Acheron's shore,
Like one whose hands are calloused by use of the mattock,
A poor man of poor parents who mourns his penurious lot.
Many the serfs who drew their allowance of rations
Monthly in the halls of Antiochos and King Aleuas;
Many the calves that were driven with the horned cattle,
Bellowing, to the Scopadian stables;
Countless the prize sheep shepherds pastured out in the open
On the plain of Crannon for the large-handed Creondae;
But no enjoyment of them remained when they had dispatched
The sweet spirit to the broad raft of the hateful old man;*
And, having taken leave of their manifold blessings,
Long ages would they have lain forgotten among the miserable dead,
If a godlike singer from Ceos,† in verse ever changing
Sung to the many-stringed lyre, had not made them famous to men
Of later days; the swift horses that returned to them wreathed
In triumph from the sacred games also won honor.

* Charon, who ferries the souls of the dead across the Styx.

† Simonides, ca. 556–468 B.C., one of whose patrons was Scopas, a king of Thessaly; Antiochos, Aleuas, and Creon were also kings, possibly of the same family.

Who would ever have known of the Lycian chiefs,* who of the long-haired
Sons of Priam, or Cycnos with the fair skin of a girl,
If poets had not sung of the war cries of earlier men?
Nor would Odysseus, who wandered among all mankind
A hundred and twenty months, who alive went to outermost Hades,
And escaped from the cave of the man-eating Cyclops,
Have won lasting glory; and Eumaios the swineherd,
And Philoitios at work with the cows of his herd,
And greathearted Laertes himself would have been swallowed in silence,
Had the songs of the man of Ionia† not brought them profit.
From the Muses comes good fame to men,
But the wealth of dead men is frittered away by the living.
But it's as much trouble to count the waves on the shore
When wind and the blue-green sea propel them landward,
Or to wash a mud brick clean in clear water,
As to persuade a man deluded by greed.
Farewell to the man of this kind, and may he have silver
Beyond counting, and the lust for more ever possess him,
But for my part I would choose honor and the affection
Of fellow men over any number of horses and mules.
I am in search of that mortal to whom I might come with my Muses
And find a welcome, for rough are the roads for singers who travel
Unattended by the daughters of Zeus great in counsel.
Heaven is not yet weary of ushering in the months and the years;
The wheel of Day will many times yet be turned by her horses;

* Sarpedon and Glaucos, allies of the Trojans in the Trojan war.
† Homer.

That man there will be who will have need of me as a singer,
When he has matched in deeds great Achilles or redoubtable
Ajax
On the plain of the Simoeis where stands Phrygian Ilos's tomb.
Even now the Phoenicians who live under the westering sun
At the outermost end of Libya shudder;
Already the Syracusans grasp their spear shafts by the middle,
And burden their arms with the wickerwork shields;
And among them Hiero girds himself like the heroes of old,
And a plume of horsehair shadows his helmet.
O Zeus, glorious father, and mistress Athene,
And Maiden,* who with your mother have in your ward the
great city
Of wealthy Ephyreans beside the waters of Lysimeleia,
Grant that evil necessities may drive our foes from the island
Down the Sardinian wave bearing tidings of death of their loved
ones
To children and wives—out of the host a remnant easily
numbered.
And may our cities, which hostile hands have utterly wasted,
Be inhabited again by their former householders;
May they once more till fertile fields; may the countless
Thousands of sheep grown fat on the nourishing grass
Bleat in the plain, and may cattle coming in herds
To their stable at twilight hasten the wayfarer homeward.
May all the fallows be plowed for sowing when the cicada
Shrills from branches high up in the trees, keeping watch over
shepherds
At midday. May spiders spin their delicate webs
Over arms, and may even the name of the battle cry no longer
be heard.

* Persephone, daughter of Demeter.

And may bards carry the towering glory of Hiero
Over the Scythian sea and to the broad wall
Bound with bitumen wherein Semiramis reigned.*
I am but one; many another the daughters of Zeus love as well,
And may it be a care to us all to sing of
Sicilian Arethusa, her people, and Hiero the spearman.
O Graces, goddesses dear to the heart of Eteocles,
You who love Minyan Orchomenos, of old time hated by
Thebes,
If I am not summoned, I will stay here, but if one invites me,
I will pluck up my courage and go, along with our Muses.
Nor will I forsake you, for what can be lovely to man
Apart from the Graces? With them may I always abide.

* Babylon.

17

Encomium to Ptolemy

Let us begin, Muses, with Zeus, and with Zeus let us end
When we sing our songs, for he is the greatest of gods.
But of men, first, last, and in between let us praise Ptolemy,
For he excels by far all other mortals.
The heroes who of old were sired by demigods,
When they had done noble deeds found skilled bards to hymn
them,
But I, with some knowledge of eloquence, celebrate Ptolemy,
For hymns are a fitting gift even for the immortals.
A woodsman arriving on thick-wooded Ida looks all around him
To see, amid that great plenty, where to start working.
What shall I mention first among the thousands of blessings
The gods have given to honor the best of all kings?
Of his lineage, what a man was Ptolemy, son of Lagos,
To accomplish a great deed when in his heart he had fixed
On a plan such as no other man could even imagine.
The father* made him equal in honor with the blessed
immortals,
And for him in the house of Zeus is set up a gold throne;
And Alexander sits beside him in friendship,
God of the gleaming diadem, grievous to Persians,
And across from them, solidly built of unyielding adamant,
Is established the seat of Heracles, slayer of Centaurs.
There he keeps feast with the others who dwell in high heaven,

* Zeus.

Endlessly rejoicing in the sons of his grandsons,
That Zeus son of Cronos freed their limbs from old age
And that the children descended from him are known as
immortals.
For the ancestor of both was the mighty Heraclid,*
And to Heracles both lines are traced in the end.
And when he leaves the feast, being replete
With fragrant nectar, to go back home to his dear wife,
He hands to one his bow and the quiver from under his arm
And to another his knurled iron club,
And to the immortal chamber of white-ankled Hebe
They lead the bearded son of Zeus with his weapons.
And among wise women how eminent was far-famed
Berenicë,
And what a blessing was she to her father and mother.
The queen who rules over Cyprus, Dione's daughter,†
Laid on her perfumed breast her delicate fingers;
Therefore it is said that never has woman so pleased a man
As Ptolemy's wife her affectionate husband,
Yet her love for him was still greater. So might a man,
Going with love to the bed of the wife who loves him,
Confidently entrust his whole estate to his children.
But the thoughts of a woman unable to love are always on
others;
Easily does she give birth, but the children are unlike their
father.
Divine Aphrodite, among gods supernal in beauty,
She was your care. Owing to you, the matchless
Berenicë never crossed Acheron, that bourn of sighing,
For you snatched her up before she reached the dark ship

* Both Alexander and Ptolemy claimed descent from Caranos, tenth in the line of descent from Heracles.
† Aphrodite.

Of the ever grim boatman who ferries the dead,*
And set her down in your temple to share in your honors.
Mild is she to all mortals and gentle the loves she inspires,
And she lightens the sorrow of hearts filled with longing.
Dark-browed Argive princess,† man-slaying Diomedes was born
Of your union with Tydeus, the Calydonian man,
And deep-breasted Thetis bore to Peleus, son of Aiacos,
Spear-hurling Achilles, but you, valiant Ptolemy,
Were borne to valiant Ptolemy by Berenicë,
And Cos nurtured you, a baby newborn,
Receiving you from your mother when you first looked on day.
For there Antigone's daughter,‡ assailed by birth pangs,
Cried out to Eileithyia who loosens the girdle,
And she stood beside her in kindly attendance, and straightway
Eased the pain in each limb, and in the father's likeness
Was born the beloved son. Cos, beholding him, cried out with joy
And, cradling the infant tenderly in her arms, spoke:
"Blessings be yours, my child, and may as much honor be mine
As was granted to blue-verged Delos by Phoebus Apollo,
And to that end raise up in prestige the Triopian hill,§
Distributing equal favor to my Dorian neighbors,
For to lord Apollo Rhenea also was dear."
So spoke the island; and from on high a great eagle
Screamed three times from the clouds—a bird of good omen.
Perhaps even a sign from Zeus. Awesome kings
Are a care to Zeus son of Cronos, but foremost among them

* Charon.
† Deïpyle, daughter of King Adrastos of Argos.
‡ Berenicë.
§ Ancient Cnidos, now Cape Crio, a promontory in southwestern Turkey near Cos.

Is he whom he loves from his birth. Prosperity is his
In abundance, and wide is the land he rules over, wide is the
sea.
Countless lands and tribes of mankind without number
Raise crops that ripen under Zeus' beneficent rain,
But no land is as fertile as the lowland of Egypt,
Where the Nile, overflowing, soaks and breaks up the clods.
Nor is there a country with so many cities of men skilled in
labor;
Three hundred cities have been established within it,
Three thousand and three times ten thousand besides,
Twice three added to three times nine more,*
And Ptolemy rules as king over them all.
He has sheared off part of Phoenicia as well, and part of Arabia,
Syria, Libya, and the domain of the black Ethiopians.
To all of Pamphylia and to the warlike Cilicians
His word is law, and to Lycians and bellicose Carians
And the Cyclades islands; for his are the best ships
Sailing the ocean, and all the sea and the land
And the rushing rivers acknowledge Ptolemy's rule.
And about him gather multitudes of spirited horsemen
And hosts of shield-bearing warriors in flashing bronze armor.
His wealth would outweigh the riches of all other kings,
So much comes to his opulent household each day from all
quarters.
His people attend in peace to their various trades;
No enemy marching overland crosses the beast-burdened Nile
To raise the battle cry in towns not their own;
No hostile armed men spring ashore from swift ships
To make raids on Egyptian cattle;
For a man such as he is settled upon the broad plains,

* The figure, 33,333, is probably an accurate tally of the settlements in Egypt at the time, though expressed in mystical terms.

Yellow-haired Ptolemy, proficient at handling the spear,
Whose utmost concern it is as a good king
To preserve his entire inheritance and to augment it himself.
Yet in that rich house gold is not heaped up to lie useless,
As if the wealth of ever industrious ants;
Much is lavished on the shrines of the gods—
First fruits ever and other offerings besides.
Many a gift does he present to powerful kings,
Much does he give to cities, and much to good comrades.
Nor does any man with skill to raise the clear-sounding song
Come to the sacred contests of Dionysos
Who does not receive the gift his performance deserves.
Those priests of the Muses sing in praise of Ptolemy
For his benefactions, and what could be finer for a man
Blessed with prosperity than to win fame among men for great
deeds?
Even for the sons of Atreus that still remains, but the vast
treasure
They won when they seized the great palace of Priam lies
hidden
Somewhere in that darkness from which there is no more
returning.
Unique among men of old and among those whose footprints
Are still warm in the dust upon which they trod,
He has built temples fragrant with incense for his dear mother
and father,
And has set them within, beautiful in ivory and gold,
To be a help to all who dwell upon earth.
And on the reddened altars he burns many a thighbone
Of fat oxen as the months roll around,
He and his noble wife,* and no woman more ardently

* Arsinoë II, sister and second wife of Ptolemy II.

Clasps in her arms her bridegroom than she in her chamber,
Loving with all her heart her brother and husband.
So also was the sacred marriage of the immortals
Born to Queen Rhea to be rulers over Olympus,
And a single bed for Zeus' and Hera's repose
Does Iris, yet virginal, spread, her hands purified with rare
perfume.

Farewell, lord Ptolemy; I will remember you
No less than other demigods, and the words I utter, I think,
Will not be wasted on men still to come; for excellence pray to
Zeus.

18

Helen's Wedding Song

In Sparta once at the palace of yellow-haired Menelaos,
Maidens with hyacinth blossoms wreathed in their hair
Before the fresh-painted bridal chamber ordered the dance,
The first twelve of the city, the flower of Laconian women,
When the younger of Atreus' sons, having courted and won
Beloved Helen, shut himself in with Tyndareos' daughter.
All sang to one strain, and with feet interweaving
Beat out the measure, and the house rang to their hymn.

Are you getting sleepy so early, dear bridegroom?
Do your knees feel unbearably heavy? Is sleep your delight?
Were you drinking so much that you had to fall into bed?
If in such haste to get to sleep early you should sleep alone
And let the girl play with her friends beside her affectionate
mother
Till morning, for tomorrow and day after day,
Year after year, Menelaos, this bride is your own.
Happy bridegroom, a good man must have sneezed for your
success
When you came to Sparta like other princes to woo.
Alone among heroes you will be son-in-law to Cronion Zeus,
For the daughter of Zeus has come under one blanket with you,
And of Achaian women no one else of her kind treads the earth;
How wonderful the child she bears if it be one like the mother!
And we, all her companions, anointing ourselves as if men,
Compete in racing along the beaches of the Eurotas—
Four times sixty maidens, a youthful feminine band—
Not one of whom when matched against Helen is flawless.

Fair the face Dawn reveals upon her arising,
Mistress Night, and bright the spring when winter has passed;
So also shone golden Helen among us.
As a tall cypress adorns the rich field or garden
It grows in, or the Thessalian courser its chariot,
So does roselike Helen adorn Lacedaimon.
No one winds off from her basket such yarn as hers,
No one plying the shuttle at the intricate loom
Cuts from the high loom beams a web more closely woven.
Nor is anyone so skilled in stroking the lyre
In hymns to Artemis and broad-breasted Athene
As Helen, in whose eyes is all desire.
O maiden of beauty and grace, you are already a housewife.
But in the early morning we will go to the racecourse
And to the flowery meadow to gather sweet-breathing garlands,
Our remembrances of you, Helen, as poignant
As the longing of newborn lambs for the teat of their mother.
First we will plait a wreath of ground-hugging trefoil
In your honor, and hang it on a shady plane tree;
First we will draw from the silver flask the glistening oil
And let it drip to the earth under that shady plane tree;
And characters shall be carved in the bark, so a passerby
May read in Doric, "Worship me; I am Helen's tree."
  Farewell, bride; farewell, bridegroom, kin of immortals.
May Leto, nurturing Leto, give you fine children,
And Cypris, goddess Cypris, equal love for each other,
And Zeus, Cronion Zeus, prosperity without end
To pass from noble parents to noble offspring forever.
Sleep, breathing love and desire to each other's breast,
Nor forget to awake at the first light of dawn.
At daybreak we will return, when the first minstrel
Lifts up his bright-plumed neck and crows from his nest.
Hymen, O Hymenaios, rejoice in this wedding!

19

(The Honey Stealer)

A horrid bee once stung thieving Eros
As he filched honeycomb from a beehive, and pricked
The tip of each finger. In pain, he blew on his hand
And hopped about and stamped on the ground, and showed
Aphrodite
His injury, complaining that so small
A beast as a bee should cause such cruel suffering.
And his mother said, laughing, "Are you not yourself like the
bees,
That though small you too cause cruel suffering?"

20
(The Country Boy)

Eunice laughed at me when I wanted sweetly to kiss her,
And callously taunted me, saying, "Get away from me!
You, a cowherd, you want to peck at me, wretch? I haven't
learned
To kiss rustics, but to press citified lips.
You're not the one to kiss my dainty mouth—not even in
dreams.
How you stare, how you mumble, how roughly you play!
How gentle your speech, how coaxing your mode of address,
How soft the beard on your chin, how silky your hair!*
Your lips are sickening, your hands are black,
And you smell bad. Away from me, and don't soil me!"
With these words, she spat three times in her bosom,
And deliberately raked me from head to foot
With insolent eyes and her lips curled in a sneer,
And with a very ladylike air she laughed at me
With her mouth wide open and scornful. Suddenly my blood
boiled,
And at the cut my skin got as red as a rose in the dew.
And she walked off and left me. But in my heart it rankles
That the foul bitch found fault with me, for I am charming.
Shepherds, tell me the truth. Am I not handsome?
Has some god then suddenly made me another mortal?

* It is not certain that these two lines are genuine. If they are a part of the poem, the tone is sarcastic.

For up to now beauty bloomed sweetly upon me.
As ivy clings to the tree trunk, my beard hugged my chin,
And my hair curled like parsley thick on my temples,
And my forehead gleamed white above my black eyebrows;
My eyes much brighter than gray-eyed Athene's,
My mouth, moreover, softer than cheese, and from my lips
My voice flowed more sweetly than honey from the comb.
Sweet is my song, whether I play on the syrinx
Or whistle a tune on the pipe or the reed or the cross flute,
And all the women up on the mountain say I'm good-looking
And all of them kiss me. But that city girl wouldn't kiss me,
But heedlessly passed me by for being a cowherd.
Doesn't she know that Cypris went mad for a herdsman*
And pastured a herd in the mountains of Phrygia? And in an
oak wood
She loved Adonis, and in an oak wood she mourned him.
And who was Endymion? Was he not a cowherd? Yet Selene
Loved that herdsman, and from lofty Olympus
Came down to the dells of Latmos to sleep with the boy.
And you, Rhea,† you weep for a cowherd. Did not even you,
Cronion Zeus, become a wandering bird for a boy‡ herding
cattle?
Eunice alone could not love a cowherd,
For she is better than Cybele and Cypris and Selene.
May she never, Cypris, have a sweetheart to kiss,
Down in the city or up on the hill, but sleep lonely all night.

* Anchises, father of Aeneas.
† Here identified with Cybele, who loved Attis, a herdsman who was killed by a boar.
‡ Ganymedes.

21

(The Fishermen)

Poverty, Diophantos, alone whets the skills;
It is she who teaches men how to labor, for nagging cares
Deny even the comfort of sleep to hardworking men,
And if for a few hours of the night a man closes his eyes,
Sudden anxieties overwhelm him and put sleep to flight.
Two old fishermen had spread out a bed of dry seaweed
Within their shelter of interlaced boughs, and lay side by side,
Leaning against the leafy wall. Nearby lay the tools
Of their strenuous calling—wicker creels,
Fishing rods, hooks, weedy bait,
Lines, nets, traps and pots woven of rush,
Rope, oars, an old boat on its props;
A bit of rush matting under their heads, their clothes, their
caps:
This was all the fishermen's capital; this was their wealth.
No key, no door did they have, no watchdog; to them
All these seemed superfluous, for poverty was their guardian.
No neighbor lived near them, and outside their shelter the sea
Swam up around them and pressed hard on the land.
Selene's chariot had not yet run half its course
When familiar toil roused the fishermen and, brushing sleep
From their eyes, they urged their drowsy minds into speech.

ASPHALION

They're liars, friend, all those who said the nights
In summer grow short when the days they bring in become
long.

I have already had ten thousand dreams, and it's not even dawn.
Or am I wrong in thinking the nights are so long?

HIS COMRADE

Asphalion, do you complain of the lovely summer?
The season has not gone out of her natural course,
But care cuts short your sleep and makes night seem long.

AS: Do you know how to read dreams? I had a good one,
And I wouldn't want you not to share in my vision.

CO: As with the catch, equal shares with all dreams.
For if I make a guess as my wits lead me,
That judge of dreams is best whose common sense is his teacher.
Besides, it passes the time, for what can one do
Lying here in the leaves by the waves if one is not sleeping?
But the ass in the thornbush, the lamp in the Prytaneum*—
These they say never sleep. But come, tell me
What the dream was tonight you would share with your comrade.

AS: When I fell asleep last evening after our day's work on the sea—
And I hadn't eaten too much, for we ate early,
If you remember, and spared our stomachs—I saw myself
Up on a rock, and there I sat on the lookout
For fish, dangling the deceiving bait from my rod.
And some big fish rose to the bait—for in sleep
Every dog dreams of his quarry, and I do of fish.
It took the bait and was hooked and the blood flowed,
And in my hands the rod bent under its thrashing.
My arms strained and flexed under the weight, and I was perplexed
How to land that great fish with my weak irons.
Then I pricked it lightly to put it in mind of its hurt

* The town hall of Athens, sacred to Hestia, or Vesta.

And slackened the line, but it didn't run, so I hauled the line
tight.
I won the fight, and my prize was a golden fish,
Thickly encrusted all over with gold. I was terrified
That the fish might be especially dear to Poseidon
Or a cherished treasure of sea-green Amphitrite.
I gently loosened it from the hook
Lest the barbs tear off some of the gold from its mouth,
And at last had it securely on the fair mainland.*
And I vowed nevermore to set foot on the sea,
But to stay on dry land and rule over my wealth.
With that I awoke. But now, my friend, put your mind
To the meaning, for I am afraid of the oath I have sworn.

CO: You have nothing to fear; you swore no oath—any more
Than you caught the golden fish you saw, for both were
illusions.
But if you search for these fabulous fish when waking, not
sleeping,
There is hope in your dream. Look for substantial fish,
Lest hunger and golden dreams bring your life to an end.

* The text here is hopelessly corrupt.

22
The Dioscuri

We hymn the sons of Leda and Zeus of the aegis,
Castor and Polydeuces, dreaded contender in boxing,
With thongs of oxhide strapped round the palms of his hands.
Twice do we hymn, and a third time, the children born
Of Thestios' daughter,* the two Lacedaimonian brothers,
Saviors of men on the thin edge of disaster,
And of horses maddened by war's bloody tumult,
And of ships that, defying the setting and rising of stars
In heaven, encounter turbulent gales—
Blasts that raise up a great wave on them from astern
Or from the bow, or each at its pleasure,
And send it crashing into the hold to burst through the walls
On both sides. And the sail and all the rigging
Hang torn and tangled, and heavy rain falls from heaven
With night coming on, and the broad sea crackles
Under the lashing of winds and the hard hail.
But from the very depths you haul up the ships
And their sailors, who had thought death was at hand,
And the winds at once die down and a slick calm
Falls on the sea and clouds drift here and there;
And the Bears appear, and the Asses,† and faintly between
them
The Manger, signaling that all is propitious for sailing.
O saviors both of mortals, both friendly to man,

*Leda, wife of Tyndareos, king of Sparta.
† In the constellation Cancer.

Horsemen and harpists, athletes and singers,
Shall I sing first of Castor or Polydeuces?
While my hymn is to both, of Polydeuces I will sing first.

The *Argo*, then, having escaped from the clashing rocks
And the terrible mouth of snowy Pontos, bearing the children
Dear to the gods, put ashore in the land of the Bebryces.
There, gathering from both sides, the crowd of men
Climbed down the one ladder and left Jason's ship,
And, disembarked on the wide beach out of the wind,
Spread their beds and with practiced hands kindled their fire.
But Castor of the swift horses and wine-ruddy Polydeuces
Wandered off by themselves apart from their comrades
And explored the wildwood of the mountain and all its delights.
Beneath a smooth rock they found a perpetual spring
Full to the brim with clear water, and down in its depths
The pebbles gleamed like bits of crystal and silver.
Tall fir trees grew nearby and all around
Were white poplars and plane trees and close-cropped cypress
And fragrant flowers, where fuzzy bees love to labor—
All the blossoms that at spring's waning burst forth in the
meadows.
There an enormous man was sitting out in the open,
Terrible to look on: his ears were mashed by rough fists,
His monstrous chest and broad back were as round as a sphere,
With flesh of iron, like a colossus beaten out with a hammer,
And under the tip of his shoulders the muscles in his brawny
arms
Bulged like round rocks a river, winter-swollen,
Has tumbled and polished in its great eddies.
Over his back and neck hung the skin of a lion,
Loosely tied together in front by the paws.
Polydeuces the champion was the first to address him.

POLYDEUCES

Good day to you, stranger, whoever you are. What mortals does this land belong to?

AMYCOS

How a good day when I look upon men I have not seen before?

PO: Don't be afraid. The men you see are not lawless nor were their people.

AM: I'm not afraid. It's not for you to teach me my business.

PO: Are you a savage, always so churlish and haughty?

AM: I am as you see. I didn't set foot on *your* land.

PO: If you should, you would go home with a visitor's gifts.

AM: Gift me no gifts. What's mine I keep for myself.

PO: You devil, wouldn't you even give someone a drink of this water?

AM: That you will know when thirst has blistered your lips.

PO: Would silver or some other payment persuade you? What do you say?

AM: Put up your hands and meet me man against man in a fight.

PO: Fistfighting, or also kicking the legs, but the eyes . . . ?

AM: With clenched fists, and don't spare your skill but strive to the utmost.

PO: Who is it, then, I'll confront in fighting with leather-strapped hands?

AM: You see him here—no womanish weakling. Call him The Boxer.

PO: Is there an additional prize for which we shall fight?

AM: I will be called your property, you mine if I prevail.

PO: Such terms are for the brawls of scarlet-combed gamecocks.

AM: Whether we turn out to be like gamecocks or lions,
For no other prize than this will we fight.

So said Amycos and sounded a call on a hollow conch shell,
And under the shady plane trees quickly assembled
In response to the blast the ever long-haired Bebryces.
And Castor, that eminent warrior, himself hastened off

To summon all of the heroes from the Magnesian ship.
Then the contenders strengthened their hands with thongs of
oxhide
And wound around their forearms long leather straps,
And met in the middle breathing slaughter against one another.
Then in their zeal came a stiff struggle to see
Which of the two should have the sun at his back.
Skillfully you outwitted the giant, O Polydeuces,
And the rays of the sun fell full on Amycos's face.
The challenger, angry at heart, then came forward
With threatening fists, but as he attacked, the son of Tyndareos
Landed a blow on the point of his chin. Now even more angry,
He botched the fighting and, head down, laid recklessly on.
The Bebryces shouted, and from the opposite side
The heroes cheered on strong Polydeuces,
Fearing lest somehow in so narrow a space
This Tityos of a man overwhelm him and bring about his
defeat.
But the son of Zeus,* stepping in on first this side, then that,
Cut him with alternate fists, and stemmed the assault
Of the child of Poseidon,† confident though he was.
Stupefied by the blows, he stood and spat out red blood,
And from the ranks of the heroes came a thundering roar
At the sight of the damaging wounds round his mouth and his
jaws,
And as his face swelled, his eyes narrowed to slits.
The prince, to further confound him, made idle feints
On all sides, and when he saw him befuddled,
Drove his fist into his forehead over his nose
And stripped the whole brow to the bone, and with the blow

*Polydeuces; Leda, his mother, was seduced by Zeus in the form of a swan, and of the children hatched from the egg, he and Helen were considered immortal.
† Amycos.

Amycos lay stretched on his back in the flowery clearing.
When he got back on his feet, the battle grew bitter
As each strove to slay the other with the tough thongs.
But the fists of the chief of the Bebryces aimed for the chest
And below the neck, while invincible Polydeuces
Hammered at the whole face with disfiguring blows.
The flesh of the giant collapsed as he sweated, and the big man
Soon became small; but ever more stalwart grew the limbs
Of the hero as the pace quickened, and his skin glowed.
   How, then, did the son of Zeus bring down that glutton?
Goddess, speak, for you know, and as your interpreter,
I will tell others whatever you wish in a way that will please
      you.
   Truly, Amycos, ambitious for a bold deed,
Seized in his left hand Polydeuces' left arm,
Leaning off guard to the side, and stepped forward
On his right foot and swung his broad fist up from his right
      thigh.
The blow would indeed have injured the king of Amyclae*
Had he not jerked his head aside and, with his stout fist
Sent from the shoulder, struck him below the left temple,
And from the gaping wound in his head the black blood poured
      swiftly.
Then he let fly a left to the mouth, and the close-set teeth
      rattled,
And with an ever sharper rain of blows pummeled his face
Until the cheeks were smashed in, and Amycos, senseless,
Stretched his length on the ground, and in surrender
Held up both hands, for he was near death.
Though you were the victor, you did nothing ignoble,
O boxer Polydeuces. But he swore to you a great oath,

* A town near Sparta, the home of the Dioscuri, but "king" may be an exaggeration.

Invoking from out of the sea his father, Poseidon,
That never again would he of his own will harass strangers.
So do I acclaim you, prince; but now, Castor, you will I sing,
Son of Tyndareos, lord of swift steeds, spearman of the bronze
breastplate.

The two sons of Zeus had seized the two daughters
Of Leucippos and carried them off, and the two brothers,
Lynceus and powerful Idas, sons of Aphareus,
Their betrothed bridegrooms, were in close pursuit.
When they arrived at the tomb of the dead Aphareus,
Together they all sprang from their chariots and rushed at each
other,
Burdened with their spears and great hollow shields.
But among them Lynceus shouted loudly from under his
helmet:
"Fools, why do you hanker for battle? And why so relentless
About other men's brides? Why these naked swords in your
hands?
Leucippos promised us these daughters of his
A long time ago, and this marriage was sworn to by oath.
It is not right of you for other men's wives,
With bribes of cattle and mules and other possessions,
To turn a man from his course and cheat us out of our wedding.
Often, indeed, have I myself said to you both
In your presence, though a man of few words,
'This is not, dear fellows, behavior becoming to heroes,
To court wives who already have plighted grooms.
Sparta is wide, and wide is horse-raising Elis,
And Arcadia, rich in flocks, and Achaian cities,
And Messene and Argos and the whole shoreline of Corinth.
There thousands of maidens are being brought up by their
parents

Who lack nothing of either beauty or wisdom,
And among these you could easily find brides to your liking,
For many fathers would gladly be fathers-in-law to good men,
And you are both distinguished among all the heroes,
And your fathers and all of your forefathers' blood from the
beginning.
But, friends, let this marriage of ours come to fulfillment,
And together let us put our minds to another for you.'
Much did I urge in this vein, but the breath of the wind
Carried it to the wet waves, and my words met with no favor,
For you are hard and unyielding. But even now be persuaded,
For you are both cousins of ours by the father."

. . .

[CA:]"But if your heart is set on war, and this quarrel of kin*
Must needs erupt and our spears be bathed in blood,
Idas and mighty Polydeuces, my brother,
Shall withhold their hands and abstain from the fight,
And Lynceus and I, we, the two younger brothers,
Will submit the outcome to Ares, leaving less grief
For our parents, for one slain man is enough from one house.
But the others will delight all of their comrades
As bridegrooms rather than corpses, and will marry these
maidens.
It is fitting that this great quarrel should end with small evil."
He spoke, and the god did not mean for his words to be idle.
The two older brothers by birth took from their shoulders
Their armor and laid it down on the ground, and Lynceus
advanced,
Shaking his mighty spear under the rim of his shield,
Even as Castor also brandished his spear points,
And the hairy plumes on the crests of both nodded.

* The beginning of Castor's speech is missing.

First they thrust with their spears at one another
Wherever they saw a part of the body exposed,
But before the sharp points could inflict a wound,
They were embedded in the terrible shields and the spears
snapped.
Then they both drew their swords from their scabbards and
tried once again
To bring death to the other, and no respite was there in the
fighting.
Many a time did Castor prick the broad shield and helm topped
with horsehair;
Many a time did Lynceus of the unerring eyes nick the shield
Of the other, and his blade grazed the red crest.
But when he aimed a swipe at Castor's left knee,
Castor stepped back and with his sharp sword lopped off his
fingers,
And Lynceus dropped his sword and to escape
Quickly ran to his father's tomb, where powerful Idas
Lounged, looking on at the battle of kinsmen.
But the son of Tyndareos rushed swiftly after
And plunged his broad sword deep into his belly and navel, and
the entrails
Within were straightway severed by the bronze blade, and
Lynceus,
Nodding, lay down on his face, and heavy the sleep that sped to
his eyes.
But Laocoösa saw not even the other one of her sons
At the paternal hearth, the happy marriage accomplished.
Messenian Idas swiftly tore up the slab
That stood to memorialize Aphareus' grave,

Meaning to hurl it at the man who had slain his brother,
But Zeus intervened and struck the carved marble out of his
hands,
And with a flaming thunderbolt turned him to ashes.

It is no light matter to fight with Tyndareos' sons;
They are strong and from a strong sire are descended.
Farewell, children of Leda, and noble renown
May you ever send to our hymns. Dear are all bards
To the sons of Tyndareos and to Helen and to the other heroes
Who helped Menelaos to topple Ilion's walls.
Your glory, lords, did the bard of Chios* contrive
In singing the city of Priam and the Achaian ships
And the fighting around Troy and Achilles, tower of the war
cry.
I too bring you an offering of the clear-toned Muses,
Such as they grant and I of myself can provide,
For songs are the loveliest honors to tender the gods.

* Homer. He merely mentions the Dioscuri. Their only connection with the Trojan war is as Helen's dead brothers.

23

(The Lover)

A man was heartsick for love of a coldhearted boy,
A youth lovely in form but unlovely in manner.
He hated his lover and displayed no tenderness for him,
Nor had he an inkling how great a god Eros was, how mighty
The bow in his hands, how cruel the arrow he shoots to the
heart;
And immune was he to all words and tender approaches.
No consolation for the fires of love was there, nor quiver
Of lip or brightening of eyes or blush on the cheek;
No word, no kiss to assuage love's desire.
As a beast of the woodland warily eyes the huntsman,
So did he mistrust every man. Savage the curl of his lip,
And his baleful eyes struck the beholder with terror.
In anger his countenance changed, and the color fled
From his face in his insolent rages. Yet even so
Was he beautiful, and his wrath enkindled his lover yet more.
But at last he could no more endure Cytherea's hot flame,
And he went to the hateful dwelling and wept cruel tears
And kissed the doorpost and raised up his voice:
"Savage and sullen boy, whelped by a foul lioness,
Boy of stone and unworthy of love, I have come
Bearing to you this last gift, my noose. No longer, lad,
Would I torment you by the sight of me. I go now
To where you have condemned me, to where people say can be
found
The drug to cure the common sorrows of lovers, oblivion.

But even if I take it to my lips and drink every drop,
My yearning will not thus be quenched. But now at last
Here on your doorstep I am content. I know what will be.
The rose too is lovely, but with time it withers away,
The violet is lovely in spring but rapidly ages;
White is the lily, but it fades when its flowering is over,
White is the snow, but it melts when it falls to the ground.
And lovely is a boy's beauty for but a short time.
There will come a day when you too will love
And with a burning heart weep bitter tears.
But, boy, do me this one last sweet service:
When you come out and see this suffering mortal
Hanging in your doorway, don't hurry past,
But stop and weep for a moment, and with your libation
Of a tear, take me down from the rope and cover me
With the cloak round your shoulders, and give me one final
kiss—
Favor my corpse at least with your lips. Have no fear of me;
I can do you no harm, and with a kiss you will rid yourself of
me forever.
And dig me a grave where my love for you will be hidden,
And as you leave, call out to me thrice: 'Dear friend, lie in
peace!'
And if you are willing, this too: 'With him, love and beauty
have perished.'
And write these letters I now inscribe on your wall:
'Love killed this man. Wayfarer, pass him not by,
But pause briefly and say, "His loved one was heartless." ' "

So saying, he picked up a stone and positioned it by the wall
At the midpoint of the threshold—an ominous stone—
And made fast the slender cord and slipped the noose round his
neck,
Then kicked out the stone from under his feet, and hung down

A dead thing. When at length the boy opened his door and saw
the corpse
Hanging from his own lintel, his heart did not falter,
Nor did he weep for the death newly wrought, but brushed by
the body,
Defiling all his youthful attire, and calmly proceeded
To the gymnasium and its games and made for the favorite pool
And the god he had insulted.* From its stone base
He dived into the water, but the statue above him
Leapt too and fell on that cruel youth and killed him.
The water turned red, and a boyish voice floated over the
surface:
"Lovers, rejoice, for he who hated is slain;
You who hate, be merciful, for the god knows how to deal
justly."

* A statue of Eros at the edge of the swimming pool.

24
The Young Heracles

When Heracles was ten months old, Midean Alcmene,
Having bathed him and Iphicles, a single night younger,
And fed both babies until they were drowsy with milk,
Put them to bed in the bronze shield, the fine armor
Amphitryon had taken as booty when Pterelaos had fallen.
The mother stroked the heads of the children and said,
"Sleep, my babes, the sweet sleep from which one awakes;
Sleep, darling souls, two little brothers, sleep safely, children;
Happily may you slumber and happily welcome the dawn."
As she crooned, she rocked the great shield, and sleep overtook
    them.
But at midnight when the Bear swings to the west
Down toward Orion, and his mighty shoulder emerges,
Hera, ever resourceful, let loose two fearful monsters,
Serpents rippling in steely blue coils,
On the broad sill in which were embedded the doorposts
Of the house, and ordered them to devour Heracles, recently
    born.
And, uncoiling, they writhed on their ravening bellies
Over the ground, and an evil fire burned in their eyes
As they approached, and they spat out deadly venom.
But when with flickering tongues they drew near the infants,
Alcmene's dear children awoke, for all things are known
To Zeus, and light sprang up all through the house.
Iphicles, as soon as he sighted the horrible beasts
Over the hollow shield, and saw their cruel fangs, started
    screaming,

And with his feet kicked away the thick blanket,
Frantic to flee; but Heracles faced them and with his hands
Bound them both in an unyielding grip,
Seizing the throat where lies the dread venom
Of deadly serpents, hateful even to gods.
They by turn wrapped their coils round the child
Lately born, still a suckling, never knowing a tear,
And again with great agony loosened their spines,
Attempting to find deliverance from that unmerciful grip.
Alcmene, hearing the cry, was first to awake.
"Get up, Amphitryon, for terror clutches me and I tremble!
Get up, and don't stop for sandals under your feet.
Don't you hear how the younger baby is crying?
Haven't you noticed that though it's still darkest night,
All the walls can be seen as clearly as if at full dawn?
There is mischief afoot in the house—there is, dear husband,
I'm certain!"
So she spoke, and at his wife's urging he jumped out of bed
And hurriedly reached for his magnificent sword
That always hung on a peg above his bed's cedar headboard.
He stretched out one hand for the new-woven baldric, and with
the other
Lifted the mighty lotus-wood scabbard.
But just then the spacious room was again filled with darkness.
He shouted out to the slaves, who in deep slumber were
snoring,
"Bring light, my slaves—get fire from the hearth—as fast as you
can,
And force back the strong bolts on the doors!"
"Wake up, you stouthearted slaves, the master is calling!"
Cried the Phoenician woman who slept by the grain mills.
And the slaves hastened forth as soon as their lamps were alight,
And the house was presently full of scurrying people.

But when their eyes fell on Heracles, that milk-fed nursling,
Tenaciously gripping the two beasts with his delicate hands,
They cried out in horror. But he held out the snakes to show to
his father,
Amphitryon, and bounced up and down in boyish delight,
And with an exultant laugh laid at the feet
Of his father those frightful monsters now cut down by death.
Alcmene caught Iphicles to her comforting bosom,
For the child was overwrought and exhausted by terror,
But Amphitryon tucked the other boy under his blanket
Of lamb's wool and went back to bed, mindful of sleep.
The cocks for the third time were announcing the breaking of
day
When Alcmene summoned Teiresias, the seer who ever spoke
truth,
And told him of the untoward occurrence,
And urged him to reveal what the outcome would be.
"And if the gods intend some hardship, don't hide it
Out of consideration for me. For to mortals
There is no escape from the thread Fate twirls from her spindle.
Seer, son of Eueres, I teach you what you well know."
So much the queen said, and he in reply answered thus:
"Be of good cheer, mother of noble children, of Perseus' blood,
Be of good cheer, and lay up in your heart the better of what is
to come.
For by the sweet light of my eyes long since departed,
Many an Achaian woman, as on her knee
She rubs the soft yarn with her hand, will sing in the evening
The name of Alcmene, and you will be honored among Argive
women.
So great a man is your son destined to be
That he will ascend to starry heaven, a hero broad-chested,
Stronger than all wild beasts and all other men.

After performing twelve labors, he will abide with Zeus
evermore,
All that is mortal consumed on a pyre in Trachis,
And he will be called the son-in-law of immortals even by those
Who stirred up the torpid beasts from their lair to end the babe's
life.*
But, woman, let there be fire ready under the ashes,
And dry fuel at hand of brierwood branches or thornwood
Or brambles or withered and wind-tossed wild pear.
And burn the two serpents at midnight on the wild firewood,
At the hour they themselves would have brought death to your
child.
In the early morning, have one of your maids gather up all the
ashes
And carry them over the river to the cleft rocks
Outside the boundaries and throw them away,
And return without looking back. And fumigate the house
First, burning pure sulfur, and then, as is the custom,
Mix salt with clear water and sprinkle it with a twig wreathed
with wool;
And sacrifice to Zeus the almighty a young male pig
That you may always be masters of those who would harm
you."
So said Teiresias and pushed back his ivory chair
And departed, burdened by the weight of his years.
But Heracles under the eye of his mother grew like a young
tree
In the orchard, and was called the son of Argive Amphitryon.
The old hero, Linos, the son of Apollo, taught the boy letters,
An ever watchful guardian over his charge;
And from Eurytos, heir to wide ancestral acres,

* Two interpolated lines have been omitted.

He learned to bend the bow and send the shaft to its target.
But Eumolpos, the son of Philammon, made him a bard,
Molding his hands to the art of the boxwood phorminx.
And all that is known to the hip-twisting wrestlers of Argos
Of how to throw an opponent by using the legs; as many tricks
As boxers, terrible in their thongs, and pancratiasts*
Who hurl themselves to the ground, have perfected to further
their craft—
All this he learned from the son of Hermes, his teacher,
Harpalycos of Panopeus, whom no one, even viewing him
From afar, would with confidence wait to oppose in a contest,
So forbidding the scowl on his grim face.
But Amphitryon himself with loving care taught his son
How to drive horses yoked to the chariot and safely
Guard the hub of the wheel as they rounded the turn,
For in horse-grazing Argos many a prize had he won
In the swift races, nor did any chariot he ever mounted
Break up until in the passage of time the straps slackened.
But to tilt at a man with couched spear, keeping the shoulder
Behind the shield, and endure light cuts of the sword,
To marshal the battle line and measure the strength of the foe
As it advanced, and to command a cavalry squadron—
This he learned from Castor, son of Hippalos, exiled from
Argos,
For Tydeus had taken possession of all his estate and wide
vineyards
In Argos, land of swift horses, receiving them once from
Adrastos;
But among the demigods there was never another such warrior
As Castor until his youth was erased by old age.

* Athletes skilled in both boxing and wrestling.

Such was the training provided for Heracles by his dear mother.
But at night the boy slept near his father, his bed
The skin of a lion, which greatly tickled his fancy.
His evening meal was of roast meat and, in a basket,
A great Dorian loaf—more than enough for a laboring man—
But by day he ate sparingly of cold victuals,
And the simple garment he wore just covered his knees.*

* The thirty-two concluding lines of the poem are too fragmentary to be intelligible.

25

(Heracles the Lion-Killer)

HERACLES AND THE COUNTRYMAN

Then the old man who looked after the cattle addressed him,
Pausing in the work on which his hands were engaged:
"Willingly, stranger, will I answer all of your questions,
For I fear retribution from Hermes, god of the highways,
Who of those whose home is in heaven they say is most angered
If anyone refuses a traveler inquiring the way.
The thick-fleeced flocks of King Augeias, who reigns in this
land,
Do not all feed in one pasture or in the same place;
Some of them graze on opposite banks of the Helison,
Some by sacred Alpheus' holy stream,
Some in Buprasion, rich in grapes, and still others here;
And there are separate folds for each of these flocks.
But for all of the herds, no matter how many,
There is always abundant pasturage here
By the great mere of Menios, for the meadows
And moist marshland provide as much sweet-tasting fodder
As is needful for building the strength of horned cattle.
But all their stables can clearly be seen over there
On your right, on the other side of the flowing river,
Stranger, where the plane trees grow close together,
And the pale wild olive—a sacred shrine
Of Apollo the Shepherd, the god who most often brings to
fulfillment.
And nearby are the roomy quarters that house the field hands,

We who zealously guard for the king his immeasurable wealth,
Sowing the seed on fallow land three times plowed under,
And often enough even turned under a fourth time.
The boundaries are known to the hardworking men of the
vineyard,
But at summer's end they all come in to the wine vats,
For this whole plain belongs to farsighted Augeias—
Wheat-bearing acres and fields and orchards of trees,
To the farthest reaches of Acroreia abounding in springs,
Where all day long we go about our various tasks,
For such is the lot of serfs who live in the country.
But tell me—for it will be to your own advantage—
What business have you in hand that you have come here?
Is it Augeias you seek or one of the bondsmen
Who serve him? For I am fairly knowing
And will tell you everything, since you are not meanly born,
I would say, nor do you seem a bad fellow yourself,
So large and imposing your build. Truly, among mortal men
So appear the children of the immortals."
And to him the strong son of Zeus said in reply:
"Yes, old man, it is Augeias, chief of the Epeians,
I would see, and my need of him is precisely why I have come.
But if he remains in the city among the townsmen
Concerning himself with their welfare while they weigh matters
of justice,
Then, old sir, lead me to one of his servants,
Whoever ranks highest in authority on the estate,
With whom I may speak and from whom in turn I may learn,
For god has decreed that mortals have need of each other."
And the good old plowman again answered him, saying:
"Stranger, you come here under the guidance of an immortal,
So quickly is accomplished all you desire.
For yesterday Helios' dear son Augeias arrived here

With his son, the noble Phyleus, mighty in strength,
Leaving the city after many a day
To look over the countless possessions he has in the country.
For even kings, I suppose, believe in their hearts
Their estate is safer when they see to it themselves.
But we'll go to him at once. I'll show you the way
To our stables, where we'll no doubt find the king."
So speaking, he led the way, but in his mind wondered much,
As he eyed the skin of the beast and the massive club in his hand,
Where the stranger had come from. He was ever longing to ask,
But, shrinking, caught back the word as it came to his lips,
Lest to his speeding companion his speech be untimely,
For it is not easy to know another man's mind.
And the dogs quickly sensed their approach from afar
By their odor as well as the tread of their feet,
And, barking excitedly, converged from all sides upon Heracles,
Amphitryon's son; but on the farther side
They fawned on the old man with harmless yelps, wagging their tails.
But by merely picking up stones from the ground,
He frightened them off, and in a harsh and threatening voice
Scolded them all and silenced their barking,
Thankful at heart because they guarded the stables
When he was away, and he then said a few words:
"By heaven! What a beast this is that the ruling gods have created
To be a companion to man—so quick to react!
If the wits within him were of the same order,
And if he knew with whom he ought to be angry and with whom not,
No other creature would match him for honor,

But now he is altogether too cross and savage."
He spoke, and they hurried along and soon reached the stables.

THE INSPECTION

Helios then turned his horses westward,
Leading the day on to evening, and the fat sheep
Came home from the pasture to sheepfolds and farms.
But the cattle, herd upon herd in countless thousands,
As they approached had the appearance of rain clouds
Rolling forward through heaven, propelled by the force
Of the south wind or the north wind from Thrace.
Without number, without end, they advance through the air,
For as many as roll along in the forward ranks
Driven by the wind, more and yet more crest up in the rear:
So always did the herds of cattle press on from behind.
The whole plain and every path was filled
With the homecoming livestock, and the rich fields rang
With bellowing, and the stables were quickly crowded
With lumbering cattle, and the sheep settled down in their
folds.
Then not a man in all that vast throng
Stood idly by lacking work with the cattle,
But this one fastened clogs to his feet with straps of leather,
Smooth and well cut, and drew in close for the milking;
Another put the newborn calves under their mothers
To drink the warm milk for which they eagerly thirsted;
One held the milk pail, another set the rich cheese,
And another led the bulls into their pens away from the females.
And Augeias moved among all the stalls observing
The care the herdsmen gave to his possessions,
And his son and Heracles, strong and resolute,
Walked with the king as he passed among that great bounty.

Then, though the heart in the breast of Amphitryon's son
Was unstirred and his spirit was ever steadfast,
Yet much did he marvel seeing all the god's largess,
For no one would say or even believe that one man
Could own so many cattle—not even ten,
Were they as rich in livestock as all other kings.
But Helios had bestowed on his son the matchless gift
Of being richer in flocks than all other men,
And to that end fostered the health and increase of the herds;
For never did dread disease visit his cattle,
Such as brings to naught the labor of herdsmen,
But ever more, ever better horned beasts filled the stalls
As year followed year, for all the cows had live births
And bore female calves in disproportionate numbers.
But three hundred bulls white-shanked and crumpled of horn
Roamed the range with the cows, and in addition two hundred
With red hides, and all were of age now to mate.
And among them grazed twelve others sacred to Helios;
Their coats shone so brightly they looked like white swans,
Distinctly visible amid all the shambling-hoofed kine,
And they grazed apart from the herd on the lush grass
In the meadow, priding themselves exceedingly on their state.
And whenever swift beasts made a foray from the dense oak
wood
On account of the cattle that grazed on the plain,
These were the first to scent them and advanced to the fray
Bellowing fiercely and with murderous aspect.
Foremost in strength and power and courage among them
Was mighty Phaëthon, whom all the herdsmen
Thought like a star, so conspicuously did he shine
As he moved among the rest of the cattle.
Now when he saw the dry skin of the terrible lion,
He made a rush at Heracles, ever watchful,

Launching his powerful head and brow at his ribs.
But the lord swiftly grasped his left horn with his thick hand
As he approached, and bent his neck to the ground,
Massive as it was, and pushed him away
With the might of his shoulder, and over the straining sinews
The muscles of his upper arm bulged straight up.
And King Augeias himself and his illustrious son
Phyleus, and the herdsmen who tended horned cattle,
Marveled to see the prodigious strength of Amphitryon's son.

[THE FIRST LABOR]*

Then, leaving behind the rich fields, together
Phyleus and mighty Heracles set off for the city.
They first sped on swift feet along the narrow path
That led away from the farm and stretched through a
vineyard—
Hardly visible among the green growth—
And when they stepped out upon the well-traveled highway,
The dear son of Augeias addressed the scion of Zeus
In the highest, who followed along close behind him,
Slightly turning his head past his right shoulder:
"Stranger, long ago I heard a tale about you—
If it was about you—and just now it comes back to my mind.
For a man arrived from Argos—I was then still a boy—
An Achaian from Helike that lies by the sea,
And he told a story—and to many other Epeians too—
About how in his presence† some Argive had killed
A wild beast, a terrible lion, a curse to the countryfolk,
Who had a hollow lair by the grove of Nemean Zeus.

* Heading added. In the text a blank line precedes the third part.
† Doubtless a raconteur's device—"I was there, I saw it with my own eyes"—to lend credibility to an incredible story.

'I don't rightly know whether he was from holy Argos itself
Or lived in the city of Tiryns or in Mycenae'—
So the man said. But he told us he was descended—
If indeed I still remember correctly—from Perseus.
I am convinced that no other Achaian* but you
Could have performed such a deed, and the skin of the beast
Slung over your ribs clearly proclaims a great labor.
Now, hero, come tell me first, that I may know in my heart
Whether I have divined truly or not,
And if you are indeed that one of whom, as we listened,
The Achaian from Helike spoke, and I have gauged you aright.
Tell me how you killed that dreadful beast single-handed,
And how it got to the well-watered countryside of Nemea.
For in all Apia you would not find such a monster,
Not if you longed to, for it does not support a beast of that kind,
But only bears and boars and the fierce tribe of wolves.
Those who heard the tale at the time were astonished,
And some even claimed that the wayfaring stranger was lying,
Endeavoring with idle chatter to entertain those around him."

So speaking, Phyleus swerved to the side of the road
That there might be room for them to walk on together
And that he might more easily hear Heracles' story.
And Heracles, coming abreast, spoke to him in these words:
"Son of Augeias, the answer to your first question
You have yourself very rightly and readily guessed.
But about this monster I will tell you in detail
How it all happened—since you are eager to hear—
Except where he came from, for that none of the Argives,
Many of them as there are, could with certainty say,

* In the text the word is *Aigialēōn*, meaning "by the sea," another name for Achaian, or for Greeks in general.

But our guess is that one of the gods whose sacrifices were
slighted
Sent this plague against Phoronean men.
For, like a river overflowing, the insatiable lion
Ravaged the whole plain, but the Bembinians most of all,
Who were neighbors of his and whose suffering was not to be
borne.
This was the first task Eurystheus set for me to accomplish,
Ordering me to kill that terrible beast.
So off I went with my pliant bow and hollow quiver
Well filled with arrows, and in my other hand clutching a club
Of close-grained wild olive—heart, bark, and all—I had shaped
From a spreading tree I found on holy Helicon
And wrenched up with its tangled roots from the ground.
But when I arrived at the place where the lion was lurking,
I grasped my bow and slipped the bowstring up to the curved
notch,
And at once fitted a lethal arrow upon it.
Then I looked around in every direction
Hoping to see the baneful monster before he saw me.
It was already midday, yet so far I had not been able
To pick up his tracks, nor had I heard any roaring.
There wasn't a man to be seen tending cattle or working
Among those furrows ready for sowing whom I might ask,
But pale terror held every soul to his dwelling.
Without staying my feet, I searched the hill thick with leaves
Until I saw him, and straightway made trial of my strength.
It was toward evening and he was approaching his cave
After gorging himself on flesh and gore, and his shaggy mane
And fierce visage and chest were all spattered with blood,
And he was licking his chops clean with his tongue.
I quickly dived for cover among the dense shrubs

Along the woodland path and lay in wait,
And as he drew near shot an arrow at his left flank,
But in vain, for the barbed shaft failed to enter the flesh,
And dropped harmlessly on the green grass.
Startled, he swiftly raised his tawny head from the ground
And with glaring eyes looked all around
And, jaws open wide, bared his ravening teeth.
Then I loosed another shaft from the bowstring,
Vexed that the first had fled from my hand to no purpose,
And hit his chest in the middle where the lungs lie.
But not even then did the painful arrow sink into his hide,
But rebounded and fell harmlessly at his feet.
Thoroughly disgusted at heart, I was preparing
To draw the bow for the third time when the beast, peering
wildly about,
Saw me and wound his long tail around his hindquarters,
At once determined on battle. His whole neck
Swelled with rage, and his tawny mane bristled
In anger, and his back arched like a bow
As he gathered his whole body back to his flanks and his loins.
As when a chariot maker, skilled at numerous tasks,
Bends a branch of wild fig, easily split,
Warming it first in the fire, into wheels for a chariot's axle,
And the smooth strip in bending slips from his hands
And springs with a single leap far away,
So that terrible lion sprang at me from afar
Intending to devour me. But I, holding my arrows
And the double cloak from my shoulders in one hand before me,
With the other raised my dry club high over my head
And drove it down on his skull, and I broke that tough olive
Club clean in two on the shaggy head
Of that invincible beast. But before he could reach me,
He fell in mid-leap to the ground, and stood on unsteady feet

Shaking his head, for the force of the blow on the bone
Had addled his brain and darkness clouded both eyes.
I saw he was fuddled by unendurable pain,
And, seizing my chance before he recovered his senses,
Threw my bow and tooled quiver down on the ground
And grabbed at the nape of that unyielding neck.
With all the strength of my sturdy hands I strangled him
From behind, lest he should rip my flesh with his claws,
Bearing down hard with my heels to keep his hind feet on the
ground
And encircling his ribs with my thighs,
Until I lifted his lifeless body upright in my arms
And stretched it out, and monstrous Hades received his spirit.
Then I gave thought to how I might skin that dead beast
And separate the rough hide from his limbs—
A difficult job, for neither with iron
Nor stone nor wood, though I tried, was I able to cut it.
Then some immortal put in my head the idea
Of tearing the lion's skin with his own claws.
Thereupon I swiftly flayed him and girded the hide about me
As a protection against the flesh wounds of battle.
So that, my friend, was the fate of the Nemean lion,
Who earlier brought much destruction to flocks and to men."

26
The Bacchantes

Ino and Autonoë and Agave, whose cheeks were like apples,
Themselves being three, led three bands of celebrants to the mountain.
Gathering wild leaves from the rough oak trees
And living ivy and asphodel that springs from the earth,
They set up twelve altars in the untrodden meadow,
To Dionysos nine, to Semele three.
They took from the mystic chest the holy offerings they had prepared
And arranged them reverently on the altars decked with fresh leaves,
As Dionysos had taught them and as he himself finds pleasing.
But Pentheus was watching them all from a steep rock,
Hidden in an old mastic tree that was growing nearby.
Autonoë saw him first and let out a terrible shriek
And with a sudden flash of her feet scattered the sacrifice
Of manic Bacchos, things not for the profane to see.
Maddened herself, straightway the others were maddened.
Pentheus fled in terror, but they pursued him
With their skirts pulled up over their knees through the cords round their waist.
Pentheus cried, "Women, what are you meaning to do?"
And Autonoë answered, "That you will know before you hear it!"
With a bellow like the roar of a lioness over her cubs,

His mother* herself seized the head of her son,
And Ino, with her foot braced on his stomach,
Tore off his great shoulder and shoulder blade, and Autonoë did
the same.
And the other women divided among them the rest of his flesh,
And, fouled with blood, they all went back to Thebes,
Bringing from the mountain not Pentheus but sorrow.†
I don't care; nor need another take thought
For one hateful to Dionysos, even if a worse fate befall him
And he be nine years of age or going on ten.
But may I myself be holy and pleasing to those who are holy.
So has the eagle honor from Zeus, aegis-bearer.
The better lot falls to the children of piety, not to impious ones.
Farewell, Dionysos, born on snowy Dracanos,
Where Zeus in the highest opened up his great thigh and
released you;
And farewell to lovely Semele and to her sisters,
Daughters of Cadmos, by many heroines honored,
Who, spurred on by Dionysos, accomplished this deed
Wherein is no blame. Let no one question the ways of the gods.

* Agave.
† There is an untranslatable pun here on "Pentheus" and "*penthēma*," meaning "lamentation" or "mourning."

27

(Love Talk)

. . . *

GIRL

Paris, another herdsman, carried off prudent Helen.

DAPHNIS

Rather did Helen seduce that herdsman with kisses.

GI: Don't be conceited, young satyr. Kisses are empty, they say.

DA: But even in empty kisses there is sweet gladness. [*Kisses her.*]

GI: I wipe off my mouth and spit out the kiss.

DA: Do you wipe your lips? Here, let me kiss them again.

GI: You ought to kiss your fine calves, not an unmarried maiden.

DA: Don't be conceited, for like a dream youth swiftly passes.

GI: What if I am getting older? Now I drink milk and honey.

DA: The grape will turn to a raisin, the rose will wither and die.

GI: Keep your hands off me! Not again! I'll scratch your lips!

DA: Come over here under the olive trees and I'll tell you a story.

GI: Not I! You fooled me before with your pleasant stories.

DA: Come over here under the elms and hear me play my syrinx.

GI: Play to yourself; nothing so dismal delights me.

DA: Now, now! Even you, my girl, should fear the Paphian's anger.

GI: Bother the Paphian! Artemis alone do I worship.

DA: Don't say that, lest she throw her strong net and enmesh you!

GI: Let her throw if she likes; Artemis still will protect me.

DA: Eros you cannot escape; no other maiden has ever escaped him.

* The introductory lines of the poem are missing, and there is considerable disagreement about the wording and order of several of the remaining lines.

GI: By Pan, I will escape him, but may you forever shoulder his yoke.
DA: I greatly fear he may give you to a worse man than I.
GI: Many have wooed me, but none of them melted my heart.
DA: As one of your many suitors, here I come too.
GI: But what can I do, dear? Marriage is full of trouble.
DA: No sorrow, no pain is there in a wedding, but dancing.
GI: Yes, but they say women are afraid of their husbands.
DA: They always rule them, rather. Why should women be frightened?
GI: Childbirth scares me. Eileithyia's arrow is sharp.
DA: But Artemis, your queen, helps women in labor.
GI: But I'm afraid having children will ruin my looks.
DA: But in your dear children you'll see a new dawn of youth.
GI: Well, if I consent, what worthy wedding gift would you bring me?
DA: You shall have all my herd, all my groves and my pasture.
GI: Swear that once married you won't desert me and leave me forlorn.
DA: Not I, by Pan, not even if you want me to leave you!
GI: Will you build me a bridal chamber, build me a house and steading?
DA: I will build you a bridal chamber and tend your fine flock.
GI: But my old father! Wh-what will I tell him?
DA: As soon as he hears my name he will give you his blessing.
GI: Tell me your name. Even a name often gives pleasure.
DA: I am Daphnis; Lycidas is my father and Nomaië my mother.
GI: You come of good family, but I am as wellborn as you.
DA: I know. You're Acrotima and Menalcas is your father.
GI: Show me your grove. Where do you stable your cattle?
DA: Come and see how tall my slender cypresses grow.
GI: Browse on, my goats. I'm off to look at the herdsman's estate.
DA: Feed well, my bulls, while I show the young lady my farm.

GI: What are you doing, young satyr? Why are you touching my breasts?
DA: I'm teaching these ripe apples of yours their first lesson.
GI: By Pan, I'm going to faint! Take your hand out!
DA: Courage, dear heart. Why are you trembling? So very timid?
GI: You're tumbling me into the brook and soiling my pretty dress!
DA: But see, I'll put this soft fleece down under your dress.
GI: Oh dear! You've ripped off my girdle! Why did you untie it?
DA: I dedicate to the Paphian this very first gift.
GI: Wait, wretch! Someone is coming! I hear voices.
DA: It's the cypresses gossiping together over your wedding.
GI: You're tearing my gown to shreds! I'm practically naked!
DA: I'll give you another gown—one even fuller.
GI: You promise me everything, but later you won't give me salt.
DA: Would that I could add my very soul to the gifts!
GI: Artemis, don't be cross because I no longer serve you.
DA: I'll offer a calf to Eros and to Aphrodite a cow.
GI: I came here a virgin but go back home a wife.
DA: Wife, mother, and children's nurse, a maiden no longer.

So, delighting in their supple young bodies,
They murmured together and celebrated their stolen wedding.
Then she got up and went back to attend to her flock
With eyes bashfully downcast but with joy in her heart,
And he, exultant over his wedding, returned to his bulls.

Take back your syrinx—it's yours again, lucky shepherd,
And let us have another pastoral song.

28

The Distaff

O distaff, friend of spinners, gift of gray-eyed Athene
To women thoughtful for the care of their household,
Come with us fearlessly to the glittering city of Neleus,
Where, green amid soft rushes, lies the shrine sacred to Cypris.
For our voyage there we pray for fair winds from Zeus
That we may exult in seeing our friend and in turn find a
welcome—
Nicias, holy child of the mellifluent Graces—
And you, our gift of ivory handsomely carved,
Will we deliver into the hands of Nicias' wife,
With whose aid you will spin an abundance of yarn for manly
attire
As well as the wispy transparencies women prefer.*
Twice a year might the mothers of lambs with soft fleeces
Be sheared in the meadow without alarming slim-ankled
Theugenis,
So efficient is she, so practical in her thinking.
For we would not care to offer you to the home
Of a lazy or shiftless housewife, for you are from our own
country,
And a native of the city Archias of Ephyra founded of old,
Marrow of the Trinacrian isle,† home of good men.
But now under the roof of a man highly skilled in the art

* Cos was famous for its sheer fabric.
† Sicily; the city is Syracuse.

Of medicine for averting the grievous ills of mankind
You will live in lovely Miletos among Ionian people,
So that Theugenis may win fame among women for her fine
spinning
And you forever recall to her memory her poet-friend.
"Truly, great love goes with a small gift," one might say
Upon seeing you. "From friends all things are precious."

29

Aeolic Love Poem

"Wine," dear boy, goes the saying, "accompanies truth,"
And we, being deep in drinking, perforce must be truthful.
I will tell you the thought that lies in my innermost mind:
You are unwilling to love me with all your heart.
That I know, for half of my life is worth living
Because of your beauty; all the rest is a ruin.
When you're complaisant, my day is like that of the gods;
But when you're perverse, the outlook is unrelieved gloom.
How is it right to inflict such pain on a lover?
But if a youngster will be guided by one who is older,
You would not only fare better yourself but have reason to
thank me.
Build only a single nest in one tree,
Where no predacious marauder can reach it.
As it is, you perch on one bough today,
Another tomorrow, from each one looking around for another,
And whoever, seeing you, praises your lovely face
You at once adopt as a friend of three years' duration
And demote him who first loved you to one of three days.
Toward men you seem to be fickle in the extreme;
Prefer, rather, to cling to your like as long as you live.
For thus will you be well spoken of by the townsmen,
And Eros will not have occasion to deal with you harshly—
Eros, who easily masters the heart of a man
And has made a weakling even of me, one of iron.
But by those delicate lips of yours I implore you

To remember that only a year ago you were younger,
And we all grow old and wrinkled before we can spit;
Once youth has fled it cannot be recalled,
For it wears wings on its shoulders,
And we are too slow to capture a creature in flight.
Such thoughts as these should persuade you to be kinder
And to return, love for love, my love undissembling,
So that when the beard of manhood roughens your cheeks,
Like Achilles and his friend may we be to each other.
But if you throw my advice to the winds to carry away
And say in your heart, "Why, you fool, do you annoy me?"
Though now I'd even go after the golden apples for you,
And Cerberos who guards the domain of the dead,*
Then, not even if you should call me, would I go out
To open the door, for my tedious longing would be over.

* The golden apples of the Hesperides and Cerberos refer to two of the labors of Heracles.

30

Second Aeolic Love Poem

Oh, this sickness of mine—hard to be borne, and
foredoomed!
For two months I have suffered from intermittent love for a
boy—
Passably fair, but charm to the soles of his feet,
And the smiles that play on his cheeks are of ravishing
sweetness.
Now the fever lasts a few days and for some days abates,
But soon there will be no respite even in sleep.
For yesterday as he walked by, he glanced at me from lowered
eyelids,
Too bashful to look me in the face, and he blushed,
And love took an even tighter grip on my heart,
And I went home bearing a fresh wound within me.
Calling my soul to attention, I expostulated at length:
"What are you up to again? When will this foolishness cease?
Aren't you aware that the hair on your temples is white?
It's time you considered: You're no longer young in appearance,
So don't act like those just getting their first taste of life.
Another thing too you forget: It is better as one grows older
To be a stranger to the heartaches of loving a boy.
For life speeds him along as if on the swift hooves of a deer,
And tomorrow he trims his sail for a different course,
And spends the flower of sweet youth among young
companions.
But memory lingers on in the other, and longing

Eats at his very marrow, and dreams beset him by night,
And a year is not long enough for his tiresome illness to pass."
Thus and with many another complaint did I upbraid my soul,
And it answered: "Whoever thinks to vanquish that trickster
Eros thinks to easily calculate
How many times nine are the stars overhead.
And now, whether I want to or not, I must stretch my neck
Its whole length and drag the yoke, for such, friend,
Is the will of the god who humbles even the great mind of Zeus
And the Cypriote* herself; me, a leaf that lives for a day,
Helpless before a light breeze, he lifts with a breath and bears
swiftly off."

* Aphrodite.

Glossary of Proper Names

Achaia, Achaian. Area in the northwestern Peloponnesos; the name for its natives is often used of Greeks in general.

Acharnae. Region of Attica, north of Athens.

Acheron. One of the five rivers that separate the living from the world of the dead; often used generally for death.

Achilles. Hero of the Trojan war, son of Peleus and the sea nymph Thetis; after withdrawing from the fighting for a while because of a dispute with Agamemnon, leader of the Greek forces, he killed Hector, leader of the Trojans, who had killed his best friend, Patroclos; was finally killed by an arrow in his heel, his only vulnerable spot, by Paris, the abductor of Helen.

Acis. River in Sicily at the foot of Mt. Etna; named for a youth whom Galatea loved and who was killed in a jealous passion by the Cyclops Polyphemos.

Acroreia. In Id. 25, apparently a mountainous region near Elis in the western Peloponnesos.

Acrotima. In Id. 27, a girl who tends goats.

Adonis. A beautiful youth loved by Aphrodite, killed by a boar while hunting; to settle a dispute between Aphrodite and Persephone, Zeus allowed him to divide his time between them; originally an eastern god of vegetation who dies annually and is worshiped with rites such as those described in Id. 15.

Adrastos. King of Argos and father-in-law of Tydeus, whose son, Diomedes, was a hero of the Trojan war.

Agamemnon. King of Mycenae, son of Atreus, and brother of Menelaos; commander of the Greek army in the Trojan war; his wife was Clytemnestra, Helen's sister; she and her lover, Aigisthos, murdered him upon his return from Troy.

Agave. Daughter of Cadmos, sister of Semele, mother of Pentheus, king of Thebes.

Ageanax. In Id. 7, the friend Lycidas sings about.

Agis. In Id. 14, a friend of Aischinas.

Agroio. In Id. 3, a fortune-teller.

Aiacos. Son of Zeus, father of Peleus and Telamon, king of Aegina.

Aigilia. Region near Athens famous for its figs.
Aigon. In Id. 4, a herdsman and boxer.
Aisaros. River near Croton in southeastern Italy.
Aischinas. In Id. 14, Cynisca's unhappy lover.
Aison. Jason's father, who was displaced as king of Iolcos by his brother, Pelias.
Ajax. Hero of the Trojan war, son of Telamon, and leader of the contingent from the island of Salamis; after Achilles' death, when he lost out in a dispute with Odysseus over his armor, he went mad and killed a flock of sheep, thinking them foes, and then, ashamed, killed himself.
Alcippa. In Id. 5, a girl friend of Comatas.
Alcmene. Daughter of Electryon, king of Midea, in Argos; wife of Amphitryon, Electryon's nephew; mother of Heracles and his twin brother, Iphicles.
Aleuas. A king of Thessaly, whose capital was Larissa on the Peneios River.
Alexander (356–323 B.C.). Son of Philip, king of Macedon, whose conquest of the world between Egypt and India earned him the appellation "the Great." After his death of a fever at the age of 32, in Babylon, his empire was divided among three of his generals, one of whom, Ptolemy I Soter, took control of Egypt.
Alexandria. City in Egypt at the mouth of the Nile River between Lake Mareotis and the Mediterranean Sea; founded in 332 B.C. by Alexander the Great; capital of Egypt under the Ptolemies and the cultural center of the world; the lighthouse on the island of Pharos in the harbor, completed in the reign of Ptolemy II, was one of the Seven Wonders of the World.
Alphesiboia. In Id. 3, daughter of Bias and Pero.
Alpheus. River in the western Peloponnesos near Olympia, the center of the worship of Zeus and site of the Olympic games.
Amaryllis. In Id. 3, the nymph who is serenaded; in Id. 4, a girl loved by Aigon and Battos.
Amphitrite. A sea goddess, wife of Poseidon.
Amphitryon. Nephew of Electryon, king of Midea; husband of Alcmene, Electryon's daughter; nominally the father of Heracles and his twin brother, Iphicles, though Zeus had assumed his form and begotten Heracles the night before Amphitryon's return from battle.
Amyclae. Town near Sparta in the southern Peloponnesos.
Amycos. King of the Bebryces and son of Poseidon, defeated in a boxing match with Polydeuces.
Amyntas. In Id. 7, a young friend of Simichidas.
Anapos. River near Syracuse in eastern Sicily.

Anaxo. In Id. 2, a female servant.
Anchises. Father of Aeneas, whom Aphrodite seduced while he was tending cattle on Mt. Ida, near Troy.
Antigenes. In Id. 7, a friend of Simichidas, brother of Phrasidamos.
Antigone. Mother of Berenicë; grandmother of Ptolemy Philadelphus.
Antiochos. In Id. 16, a king of Thessaly, whose glory was apparently celebrated in a poem by Simonides.
Aphareus. Father of Idas and Lynceus; brother of Leucippos and half brother of Tyndareos.
Aphrodite. Goddess of love; wife of Hephaistos; according to some accounts the mother of Eros; Cyprus was especially associated with her worship, and hence the appellations "Cypris" and "Paphian"; she loved Adonis, a youth killed by a boar while hunting, and Anchises, by whom she was the mother of Aeneas.
Apia. Another name for Argos and by extension for the Peloponnesos in general, as in Id. 25; after Apis, the son of Phoroneus, legendary king of Argos.
Apollo. God of reason, justice, prophecy, and, because of his association with the Muses, the arts. His functions overlap those of Zeus and Athene and, as the agent of sudden and untimely death, those of his twin sister, Artemis. In general, he represents the intellectual qualities of man as against the emotional, orgiastic elements represented by Dionysos. Delphi was the center of his worship. In Id. 25, he is presented as the protector of flocks.
Arabia. Peninsula in southwestern Asia between the Red Sea and the Persian Gulf.
Aratos. In Id. 6, apparently a friend of Theocritus; in Id. 7, the subject of Simichidas's song, perhaps the same friend.
Arcadia. Region in the central Peloponnesos; center of the worship of Pan.
Arcas. Son of Callisto (or Helike) and Zeus; according to one myth, Pan's brother; ancestor of the Arcadians.
Archias. A Corinthian, legendary founder of Syracuse, in eastern Sicily, in the eighth century B.C.
Ares. God of war; son of Hera and Zeus, and almost universally disliked except by Aphrodite.
Arethusa. Fountain on the island of Ortygia in the harbor of Syracuse, in eastern Sicily; named for the nymph who tried to evade the advances of the river Alpheus.
Argo. The ship in which Jason and his companions sailed to Colchis to recover the Golden Fleece.
Argonauts. Company of heroes who sailed with Jason in the *Argo* to recover the Golden Fleece.

Argos, Argive. City and region in the northeastern Peloponnesos, in the vicinity of Mycenae and Tiryns, the area now called Argolis; the name for its natives is often used for Greeks in general.

Ariadne. Daughter of King Minos of Crete, who helped Theseus to thread the labyrinth and overcome the Minotaur, but whom he abandoned on the island of Naxos, or Dia, on the return voyage to Athens.

Aristis. In Id. 7, a singer and friend of Aratos in Simichidas's song.

Arsinoë (ca. 316–270 B.C.). Sister and second wife of Ptolemy Philadelphus (his first wife and the mother of his children was also named Arsinoë); an able ruler in her own right, she was chiefly responsible for the military victories of Philadelphus's reign.

Artemis. Goddess of chastity and wild animals, twin sister of Apollo, corresponding to the Roman Diana; often depicted in a short tunic carrying bow and quiver and attended by a deer; assists women in difficult childbirth and is the agent of untimely death to women.

Asphalion. In Id. 21, a fisherman.

Asses, the. Two stars in the constellation Cancer.

Assyria. Country east of the Tigris River in western Asia.

Atalanta. A girl, reluctant to marry, who lost a foot race to her suitor, Hippomenes, and thereby became his wife, her attention distracted during the race by the golden apples he dropped at intervals.

Athene. Virgin goddess of battles, intelligence, and handicrafts, especially spinning and weaving; usually depicted wearing a helmet and carrying a spear and shield; at her birth she sprang fully armed from the head of Zeus; sometimes, as his delegate, she wears the goatskin aegis; patron goddess of Athens.

Athens, Athenian. City in Attica in the southeastern part of the Greek mainland; center of Greek culture in classical times, but eclipsed by Alexandria during Theocritus's time.

Athos. Mountainous peninsula in northern Greece.

Atreus. King of Mycenae; son of Pelops and father of Agamemnon and Menelaos.

Attica, Attic. Region around Athens in the southeastern part of the Greek mainland.

Augeias. King of Elis in the western Peloponnesos, the cleaning of whose stables was one of the labors of Heraclas; in Id. 25, the son of Helios, the sun god.

Autonoë. Daughter of Cadmos of Thebes, sister of Semele.

Bacchos. Another name for Dionysos.

Battos. In Id. 4, a goatherd.

Bear, the. The constellation Ursa Major (in Greek, *Arktos*), the Great Bear or Big Dipper.

Bebryces. Tribe on the south coast of the Black Sea visited by the Argonauts on their voyage to recover the Golden Fleece; Amycos, son of Poseidon, was their king.
Bellerophon. Grandson of Sisyphos, founder and king of Corinth, who tamed the winged horse Pegasos, killed the fire-breathing monster Chimaira, married a Lycian princess, and sired a royal family that included Sarpedon, a hero of the Trojan war.
Bembina. Village near Nemea in the northeastern Peloponnesos.
Berenicë (ca. 340–281 B.C.). Third wife and half sister of Ptolemy I and mother of Ptolemy Philadelphus and his second wife, Arsinoë; deified after her death and associated in worship with Aphrodite.
Bias. A youth who loved Pero, the daughter of Neleus, who demanded the cattle of Iphiclos as a bride price. With the help of his brother, the seer Melampus, he eventually delivered the cattle and won his bride.
Bibline. In Id. 14, a choice kind of wine; possibly imported from Thrace.
Blemyan. Pertaining to the Blemyes, a tribe living east of the Nile River on the southern frontier of Egypt, subject to the Ethiopians.
Bombyca. In Id. 10, the flute girl Bucaios loves.
Brasilas. In Id. 7, apparently an ancient hero of Cos.
Bucaios. In Id. 10, a reaper.
Buprasion. Grape-producing area in Elis in the western Peloponnesos.
Burina. A spring in Cos, not far from the famous Asclepieion.
Byblis. A spring in Miletos, named for the daughter of Miletos of Crete, mythical founder of the city.

Cadmos. A Phoenician, legendary founder of Thebes, whose daughter Semele was the mother of Dionysos; credited with introducing the alphabet into Greece.
Calaithis. In Id. 5, Lacon's mother.
Calydna. Island in the Aegean just north of Cos; now called Calymnos.
Calydon. Kingdom in Aitolia, in the southwestern part of the Greek mainland; scene of the Calydonian boar hunt and home of Tydeus.
Caranos. Descendant of Heracles and the common ancestor of Ptolemy and Alexander.
Caria. Region in southwestern Asia Minor (now Turkey) whose capital was Halicarnassos (now Bodrum).
Carnea. Harvest festival in honor of Apollo, featuring sports and music, celebrated mostly in Sparta, but adopted by other Dorian settlements.
Castalia. A spring on Mt. Parnassos near Delphi in central Greece, sacred to Apollo and the Muses.

Castor. Son of Tyndareos and Leda and brother of Polydeuces (or Pollux) and Helen; a notable horseman and fighter; one of the company of heroes who sailed in the *Argo* to recover the Golden Fleece; killed in a fight with Idas and Lynceus but shared his brother's immortality, coming to life after death every other day. In Id. 22, he survives the other twins.

———. In Id. 24, son of Hippalos of Argos, Heracles' military instructor.

Caucasus. Mountains in Russia between the Black and Caspian seas.

Ceos. Island in the Aegean southeast of Attica; one of the Cyclades; birthplace of Simonides.

Cerberos. Three-headed dog guarding the entrance to the underworld domain of the dead, whose capture was one of the labors of Heracles.

Chalcon. In Id. 7, ancestor of Phrasidamos and Antigenes.

Charon. Boatman who ferries the souls of the dead over the river Styx (or Acheron) to the realm of Hades; represented as a grim, ugly old man.

Cheiron. A Centaur, half horse and half man, renowned for his wisdom and virtue, who had as pupils Asclepios, Jason, and Achilles, among others.

Chios. Island in the Aegean off the west coast of Turkey south of Lesbos; thought by some to be the birthplace of Homer.

Chromis. In Id. 1, a Libyan singer.

Cianians. Tribe who lived in the valley of the Cios River south of the Sea of Marmara, in what is now northwestern Turkey.

Cilicia. Region in southeastern Asia Minor (now Turkey) extending along the Mediterranean coast south of the Taurus Mountains.

Cinaitha. In Id. 5, a ewe.

Circe. A sorceress who changed Odysseus's shipmates to swine after drugging them with wine.

Cissaitha. In Id. 1, a she-goat.

Clearista. In Id. 2, a friend of Simaitha; in Id. 5, a girl Comatas loves.

Cleunicos. In Id. 14, a friend of Aischinas.

Clytia. In Id. 7, ancestress of Phrasidamos and Antigenes.

Colchis. Country at the eastern end of the Black Sea, ruled by King Aietes, Medea's father, the land to which Jason and his companions sailed in the *Argo* to bring back the Golden Fleece, which was guarded by a dragon on Aietes' estate.

Comatas. In Id. 5, a goatherd; in Id. 7, a legendary goatherd and singer in Lycidas's song.

Conaros. In Id. 5, a ram.

Corinth, Corinthian. City in the northeastern Peloponnesos on the isthmus between mainland Greece and the peninsula; formerly called Ephyra; mother city of Syracuse, in eastern Sicily.

Corydon. In Id. 4, a cowherd; in Id. 5, a friend of Lacon.

Cos. Island in the Aegean off the southwestern coast of Asia Minor (now Turkey) near Halicarnassos (Bodrum); a center of learning, especially in medicine; birthplace of Hippocrates, the great physician, and of Ptolemy Philadelphus; for a time the home of Theocritus.

Cotyttaris. In Id. 6, an old wise woman.

Crannon. City on the plain south of Larissa in Thessaly in northeastern Greece.

Crathis. River in southeastern Italy near Sybaris, where there was a shrine to Pan.

Cratidas. In Id. 5, a boy Lacon loves.

Creondae. In Id. 16, a royal family of Thessaly, possibly related to Scopas, a patron of Simonides.

Crocylos. In Id. 5, a friend of Comatas.

Croesus. Sixth-century king of Lydia, in Asia Minor, whose wealth was proverbial.

Cronos. A Titan, father of Zeus and his five sisters and brothers, who swallowed his children at birth for fear one of them would overthrow him. His wife, Rhea, substituted a stone for Zeus, who, when he came to manhood, made him vomit up the other children, and after a war that raged for ten years, overthrew him and the other Titans.

Croton. Greek city in southeastern Italy.

Cybele. Ancient earth goddess identified with Rhea and worshiped especially in Phrygia; she loved Attis, a herdsman who, like Adonis, was killed by a boar.

Cyclades. Group of islands in the central Aegean, including Naxos, Paros, Myconos, and Delos, among others.

Cyclops. Mythical creature with one eye in the center of the forehead; in particular, Polyphemos.

Cycnos. Son of Poseidon who was killed by Achilles when the Greeks first landed at Troy; noted for his white complexion; his name means "swan."

Cydonia. In Id. 7, home of Lycidas, but whether in Crete or elsewhere is not known.

Cymaitha. In Id. 4, a calf.

Cynisca. In Id. 14, the girl Aischinas loves.

Cypris. Another name for Aphrodite, from her association with Cyprus.

Cyprus. Large island in the eastern Mediterranean off the southern coast of Turkey; a center of the worship of Aphrodite.

Cytherea. Another name for Aphrodite, from her association with the island of Cythera, off the southeastern coast of the Peloponnesos.

Damoitas. In Id. 6, a cowherd.

Daphnis. A Sicilian herdsman who died of love, son of Hermes, and legendary inventor of pastoral song; in Idd. 6, 8, 9, and 27, a cowherd, possibly the legendary Daphnis at an earlier age.

Deïpyle. Daughter of King Adrastos of Argos; wife of Tydeus; mother of Diomedes, a hero of the Trojan war.

Delos. Island in the central Aegean, sacred to Apollo as his birthplace; one of the Cyclades.

Delphis. In Id. 2, Simaitha's faithless lover.

Demeter. Goddess of agriculture; mother of Persephone and of Plutos, god of agricultural wealth; Eleusis was the center of her cult, but it was also important in the Dorian settlements of southwestern Asia Minor.

Deo. Another name for Demeter.

Deucalion. Son of Prometheus, who with Pyrrha, his wife, survived a flood that destroyed the rest of mankind; their eldest son was Hellen, legendary ancestor of the Hellenic race, whose sons were Doros, Xuthos, and Aiolos, legendary ancestors of the Dorians, Ionians, and Aiolians.

Dia. Another name for Naxos, one of the Cycladic islands in the central Aegean, where Theseus abandoned Ariadne, daughter of King Minos of Crete.

Dinon. In Id. 15, Praxionë's husband.

Diocleides. In Id. 15, Gorgo's husband.

Diocles. A man from Attica (possibly a ruler of Eleusis) who while in exile in Megara, on the Isthmus of Corinth, was killed in battle defending a friend; games in his honor were held in Megara.

Diomedes. Son of Tydeus and Deïpyle of Argos; hero of the Trojan war, who wounded Aphrodite when she tried to rescue her son Aeneas from the fighting.

Dione. Mother of Aphrodite; in Id. 7, another name for Aphrodite herself.

Dionysos. God of wine, representing the irrational, demonic aspects of the personality, as opposed to the rational and intellectual qualities represented by Apollo. Drama, as well as orgiastic rites, developed as a major part of his worship. He was born from the thigh of Zeus after Semele, his mother, was destroyed by lightning.

Diophantos. In Id. 21, the friend to whom the poem is addressed.

Dioscuri. The twins Castor and Polydeuces, sons of Leda and Tyndareos (or Zeus) and brothers of Helen of Sparta. The name means "sons of Zeus."

Dorian, Doric. Tribe from northwestern Europe that in the second millennium B.C. migrated south, displacing the earlier inhabitants of Greece and bringing to an end the old Mycenaean civilization. The Dorians overran most of the Peloponnesos, and in later migrations extended their influence to colonies such as Syracuse and Corcyra in the west and Cos, among others, in the southern Aegean and adjacent coast of Asia Minor. The Doric dialect, with local variations, was widely spoken, and it is the dialect in which Theocritus wrote.

Dracanos. Birthplace of Dionysos, apparently a mountain in northern Europe or Asia.

Edonians. A Thracian tribe that lived near the Rhodope Mountains, in what is now Bulgaria.

Egypt. Country in northeastern Africa whose northern boundary is on the Mediterranean Sea; Alexandria was its capital in Theocritus's time.

Eileithyia. Goddess of childbirth; daughter of Zeus and Hera.

Elis. Region in the western Peloponnesos, inhabited by the Epeians, owing its importance to the worship of Zeus at Olympia.

Endymion. A beautiful youth loved by Selene, who at the price of eternal sleep was granted immortality and perpetual youth; associated with Mt. Latmos in Caria (now western Turkey).

Eos. Goddess of dawn.

Epeians. The inhabitants of Elis, in the western Peloponnesos near Olympia.

Ephyra. Ancient name for Corinth.

Eros. God of love; according to some accounts Aphrodite's son, according to others a force in existence from the beginning of creation; often used in the plural (*Erotes*) as a bevy of winged youths or cupids armed with bows and arrows.

Eryx. Mountain on the western coast of Sicily; a center of the worship of Aphrodite.

Eteocles. King of Orchomenos, a city in Boeotia in central Greece, who established a cult for the worship of the three Graces.

Ethiopia. Country in northeastern Africa, south of Egypt.

Etna. Volcano in northeastern Sicily; also the town at its base.

Eubolos. In Id. 2, father of Anaxo.

Eucritos. In Id. 7, a friend of Simichidas.

Eudamippos. In Id. 2, a friend of Delphis.

Eueres. Father of Teiresias, the blind seer of Thebes.

Eumaios. In the *Odyssey*, a faithful swineherd who helps Odysseus kill Penelope's suitors.
Eumaras. In Id. 5, the employer of Comatas.
Eumedes. In Id. 5, a boy Lacon loves.
Eumolpos. In Id. 24, Heracles' music instructor.
Eunicë. In Id. 13, a water nymph; in Id. 20, a city girl who spurns a rustic.
Eunoë. In Id. 15, Praxinoë's servant.
Eurotas. River in the southern Peloponnesos on which Sparta was situated.
Eurystheus. King of Tiryns, in the northeastern Peloponnesos, for whom Heracles performed twelve labors.
Eurytos. In Id. 24, Heracles' archery instructor.
Eutychis. In Id. 15, Gorgo's servant.

Fates. The three goddesses, represented as spinners, who apportion the thread of human life.

Galatea. A sea nymph loved by the Cyclops Polyphemos.
Ganymedes. A beautiful boy of the royal line of Troy whom Zeus in the form of an eagle bore off to Olympus to serve as cupbearer to the gods.
Glaucë. A poet and musician from Chios who was well known in Alexandria in Theocritus's time.
Golgoi. A center of Aphrodite's worship in Cyprus.
Gorgo. In Id. 15, a housewife of Alexandria.
Graces. Goddesses, usually three in number, who personify loveliness and grace; the art of poetry is their special province, and they are friends of the Muses; in Id. 16, they personify Theocritus's poems.

Hades. God of the underworld, in whose realm, or "house," the souls of the dead are received; Persephone's husband and the brother of Zeus and Poseidon.
Haimos. Mountains in Thrace; now the Balkan range in Bulgaria.
Haleis. In Id. 5, apparently a river near Sybaris in southeastern Italy; in Id. 7, a river and district in Cos.
Harpalycos. In Id. 24, Heracles' instructor in boxing and wrestling, a son of Hermes.
Hebe. Goddess of youth; daughter of Zeus and Hera; wife of Heracles after his elevation to divinity following his death as a hero; preceded Ganymedes as cupbearer to the gods.
Hebros. River in Thrace; now the Maritsa River in Bulgaria.

Hecate. Goddess of the underworld region of the dead, of terrible aspect; associated with Persephone and Artemis, and with sorcery and crossroads.

Hector. Son of Priam, king of Troy, and a hero of the Trojan war; he killed Achilles' friend Patroclos and was himself killed by Achilles.

Hecuba. Wife of Priam, king of Troy, and mother of Hector and Paris, among others; she was carried off to Greece after the fall of Troy as a slave of Odysseus, in Thrace avenged the death of another son, and was eventually transformed into a dog.

Helen. Daughter of Leda and Tyndareos (or Zeus), celebrated for her surpassing beauty; wife of Menelaos, king of Sparta; eloped with Paris, son of Priam, king of Troy, and thus brought about the Trojan war.

Helicon. Mountain in Boeotia, in central Greece, sacred to the Muses.

Helike. City in Achaia in the northern Peloponnesos, on the Gulf of Corinth; also another name for Callisto, mother of Arcas.

Helios. The sun god, who drives his chariot across the heavens from dawn to dark; in Id. 25, father of Augeias, king of Elis.

Helison. River in Elis in the western Peloponnesos.

Hellespont. The Dardanelles, connecting the Sea of Marmara with the Aegean; named for Helle, sister of Phrixos, who fell off the golden ram and was drowned there as they flew over it in escaping to Colchis.

Hephaistos. God of fire, associated with volcanoes; artist, armorer, and craftsman of the gods; a cripple and a humorous object to his fellow Olympians; Aphrodite's husband.

Hera. Sister and wife of Zeus; goddess of marriage; plagued by her husband's constant infidelities and merciless toward her rivals; worshiped especially in Argos.

Heracles. Hero renowned for his prodigious strength; son of Alcmene and Amphitryon (or Zeus); after death he became a god and married Hebe, daughter of Zeus and Hera; performed twelve labors for King Eurystheus of Tiryns.

Heraclid. In Id. 17, Caranos, the ancestor from whom Alexander and Ptolemy claimed descent.

Hermes. God of travelers, traders, and thieves, messenger of the gods, and conductor of souls to the region of the dead; in Id. 1, father of Daphnis.

Hestia. Virgin goddess of the hearth, corresponding to the Roman Vesta; firstborn of Cronos and Rhea.

Hiero II. Tyrant of Syracuse (270–215 B.C.), who achieved military fame during Pyrrhus's Sicilian campaign by driving the Carthaginians back to western outposts in Sicily; an ally of Rome in the Punic wars; an earlier ruler of the same name was a patron of Simonides, Pindar, and Aeschylus in the fifth century B.C.

Himera. River in northern Sicily, also a city of that name; in Id. 5, apparently a river near Sybaris in southeastern Italy.

Hippalos. In Id. 24, father of Castor of Argos, Heracles' military instructor.

Hippocion. In Id. 10, a landowner.

Hippomenes. A youth who in order to win the hand of Atalanta had to defeat her in a foot race. He distracted her attention by dropping three golden apples at intervals and won both the race and his bride.

Homer. Blind poet of the eighth century B.C.; author of the *Iliad* and the *Odyssey;* thought to be a native of Chios, an island in the Aegean off the west coast of Turkey.

Homole. In Id. 7, apparently the valley of the Peneios River near Mt. Ossa in Thessaly in northeastern Greece; usually called Tempe.

Hours. Goddesses of the seasons, usually three in number, representing spring, summer, and winter; associated with Aphrodite and with dew and rain.

Hyetis. In Id. 7, apparently, like Byblis, a spring in Miletos.

Hylas. Son of Theiodamas, king of the Dryopes, whom Heracles adopted after killing his father; became immortal and was worshiped in annual rites in Mysia, in northwestern Asia Minor, near the Sea of Marmara.

Hymen, Hymenaios. God of marriage, invoked in wedding songs.

Iasion. Lover of Demeter; father of her son Plutos, god of agricultural wealth.

Icaria. Island in the Aegean west of Samos off the west coast of Turkey.

Ida. Mountain near Troy, in northwestern Asia Minor, scene of Aphrodite's seduction of Anchises.

Idalion. A center of Aphrodite's worship in Cyprus; modern Dhali.

Idas. Son of Aphareus and Laocoösa and brother of Lynceus; one of the company of heroes who sailed in the *Argo* to recover the Golden Fleece; a rival with Apollo for the hand of Marpessa, who chose him over the god.

Ilion. Another name for Troy.

Ilos. In the royal line of Trojans, great-grandson of Dardanos and grandfather of Priam; founder of the city of Troy (Ilion).

Ino. Daughter of Cadmos of Thebes, sister of Semele.

Iolcos. City on the Pagasaean Gulf in Thessaly in northeastern Greece (modern Volos); point of embarkation for the Argonauts who sailed with Jason to Colchis to recover the Golden Fleece.

Ionia, Ionian. The Greek colonies along the western coast of Asia Minor (now Turkey) from Smyrna (Izmir) to Miletos, and the adjacent islands, predominantly of Athenian or Attic origin.
Iphicles. Twin brother of Heracles, born to Alcmene and Amphitryon one night later than his brother.
Iris. Messenger of the gods, personification of the rainbow.

Jason. Son of Aison and rightful heir to the kingdom of Iolcos in Thessaly, who in order to claim his heritage sailed in the *Argo* with a band of Greek heroes to bring back the Golden Fleece of the ram on which a kinsman, Phrixos, in danger of death, had fled to Colchis. With the aid of Medea, a beautiful sorceress, he was successful in his mission, but failed to regain his kingdom.

Kids, the. Two stars in the constellation Auriga, near Capella, the bright star in the upper right-hand corner.

Labes. In Id. 14, father of Lycos.
Lacedaimon. Another name for Sparta.
Lacinia. Another name for Hera; there was a temple to Lacinian Hera in Croton, in southeastern Italy.
Lacon. In Id. 5, a shepherd.
Laconia. Region in the southern Peloponnesos; its capital was Sparta.
Laertes. Father of Odysseus.
Lagos. A Macedonian, father of Ptolemy I Soter.
Lampriadas. In Id. 4, the reference is obscure: possibly a neighbor, possibly a district near Croton, in southeastern Italy.
Lampuros. In Id. 8, a sheep dog.
Laocoösa. Mother of Idas and Lynceus; wife of Aphareus.
Lapiths. A Thessalian people who were neighbors and near relatives of the Centaurs. When their king, Pirithoös, married Hippodamia, the Centaurs, who had been invited to the feast, tried to carry off the bride and the other women, and a war resulted, in which the Lapiths were victorious.
Larissa. City on the Peneios River in Thessaly in northeastern Greece.
Latmos. Mountain in Caria (southwestern Turkey), where Endymion slept his eternal sleep.
Latymnon. In Id. 4, apparently a mountain near Croton in southeastern Italy.
Leda. Daughter of Thestios, wife of Tyndareos, and mother of Helen, Clytemnestra, Castor, and Polydeuces; Helen and Polydeuces were fathered by Zeus, who seduced her in the form of a swan.
Lepargos. In Id. 4, a calf.

Leto. Mother of Apollo and Artemis, worshiped in conjunction with them, especially in Delos.

Leucippos. Father of the girls to whom Idas and Lynceus were betrothed and whom Castor and Polydeuces abducted; brother of Aphareus and half brother of Tyndareos.

Libya. The continent of Africa; in Id. 16, Carthage.

Linos. In Id. 24, Heracles' literary instructor and guardian, a son of Apollo.

Lipara. Volcanic island off the northern coast of Sicily, sacred to Hephaistos.

Lityerses. A Phrygian, son of King Midas, who challenged men to reaping contests and killed those who lost; a harvest song is associated with him.

Lycaios. Mountain in Arcadia in the central Peloponnesos, traditionally the birthplace of Pan.

Lycaon. Father of Callisto, or Helike, mother of Arcas.

Lycia. Region of Asia Minor, on the southwestern coast of what is now Turkey.

Lycidas. In Id. 7, a goatherd and poet; in Id. 27, father of Daphnis.

Lycon. In Id. 2, a neighbor of Simaitha; in Id. 5, a friend of Lacon.

Lycopas. In Id. 5, a cowherd.

Lycope. Town in Aitolia in the southwestern part of the Greek mainland.

Lycopeos. In Id. 7, father of Phrasidamos and Antigenes.

Lycos. In Id. 14, a youth Cynisca loves.

Lydia. Region of Asia Minor north of Caria in what is now western Turkey.

Lynceus. Son of Aphareus and Laocoösa and brother of Idas; one of the company of heroes who sailed in the *Argo* to recover the Golden Fleece; notable for his preternaturally keen vision; killed in a fight with Castor.

Lysimeleia. Lake or marsh near the harbor of Syracuse in eastern Sicily.

Magnesia. Mountainous strip of land along the Aegean coast of Thessaly in northeastern Greece, north of the island of Euboea; its principal city was Iolcos, from which the Argonauts sailed.

Mainalos. Mountain in Arcadia in the central Peloponnesos sacred to Pan.

Malis. In Id. 13, a water nymph.

Manger, the. Nebula in the constellation Cancer.

Medea. Daughter of King Aietes of Colchis, a sorceress, who helped Jason to recover the Golden Fleece and who fled with him from Colchis and later married him.

Megara, Megarian. City on the Isthmus of Corinth overlooking the island of Salamis; in Id. 14, the reference is to an ancient oracle ranking it last among famous cities.
Melampus. A seer, brother of Bias, who with some difficulty delivered the cattle of Iphiclos, which Neleus had demanded as the bride price of his daughter Pero, whom Bias loved.
Melanthios. In the *Odyssey*, a goatherd who was castrated in the fight in which Odysseus killed Penelope's suitors.
Melita. Another name for Persephone.
Melixo. In Id. 2, sister of Philista and a servant of Simaitha.
Menalcas. In Id. 8, a shepherd; in Id. 9, a cowherd; in Id. 27, father of Acrotima.
Menelaos. Son of Atreus, younger brother of Agamemnon, husband of Helen, king of Sparta; his wife's abduction by Paris resulted in the Trojan war, in which he participated.
Menios. Lake or mere in Elis in the western Peloponnesos.
Mermnon. In Id. 3, the employer of a servant girl.
Messene. Region in the southwestern Peloponnesos near Laconia, frequently at war with Sparta and at one time under its subjugation.
Micon. In Id. 5, a friend of Comatas.
Midea. City in Argos in the northeastern Peloponnesos ruled by Electryon, Alcmene's father; identified with Dendra.
Miletos. Ionian city on the coast of Caria (now western Turkey), a center of trade and manufacture, noted especially for its woolen products.
Milon. In Id. 4, a trainer of boxers; in Id. 8, a youth in Menalcas's song; in Id. 10, a reaper.
Minyans. Tribe named for the legendary Minyas, father of Orchomenos and associated with the city of that name in Boeotia in central Greece.
Molon. In Id. 7, Aratos's rival in Simichidas's song.
Morson. In Id. 5, judge of the contest between Comatas and Lacon.
Muses. The nine daughters of Zeus who presided over the arts—poetry, history, music, and the dance.
Mycenae. City in the northeastern Peloponnesos, near Argos and Tiryns, ruled by Atreus and, later, his son Agamemnon.
Myndian. A native of Myndos, a city on the coast of Caria, near Halicarnassos, or what is now Bodrum in western Turkey.
Myrto. In Id. 7, the girl Simichidas loves.
Mytilene. City on the island of Lesbos, off the western coast of Turkey.

Naïs. In Id. 8, a nymph in Daphnis's song, whom he later marries.
Neaithos. River near Croton in southeastern Italy.
Neleus. Legendary founder of Miletos, who led a migration of Ionians

from Attica on the Greek mainland in Mycenaean times; also a king of Pylos, father of Nestor, a hero of the Trojan war.

Nemea. Valley near Mycenae in the northeastern Peloponnesos, site of a temple and grove sacred to Zeus, where the Nemean games were held.

Nereids. Sea nymphs, daughters of Nereus, a sea god.

Nicias. A physician and poet who was a friend of Theocritus and lived in Miletos.

Nile. River of Africa that flows north through Egypt into the Mediterranean Sea.

Nisaea. Port of Megara on the Isthmus of Corinth near the island of Salamis in the Saronic Gulf.

Nomaië. In Id. 27, mother of Daphnis.

Nychea. In Id. 13, a water nymph.

Nymphs. Lesser divinities, spirits of trees, groves, mountains, springs, streams, the sea, and other natural objects.

Ocean. The river that encircles the earth, considered a flat disk in ancient times.

Odysseus. King of Ithaca and hero of the Trojan war, who had many adventures on his ten-year voyage home, described in the *Odyssey* of Homer.

Oecos. Town in Caria (now western Turkey) near Miletos.

Olpis. In Id. 3, a fisherman.

Olympus. Mountain in Thessaly in northeastern Greece; home of the gods.

Orchomenos. City on Lake Copais in Boeotia in central Greece, renowned in Mycenaean times for its wealth, destroyed by Thebes in the fourth century B.C.

Orion. A constellation depicting a hunter, with one bright star in his right shoulder, one in his left foot, and three closely spaced stars in a diagonal line forming his sword belt.

Oromedon. In Id. 7, apparently a mountain in the range along the southern coast of Cos.

Othrys. Mountain in Thessaly in northeastern Greece.

Paean. Another name for Apollo; also a hymn in his praise.

Pamphylia. Region on the southern coast of Asia Minor (now Turkey) east of Lycia.

Pan. Mischievous, goatlike god of flocks, often represented as playing the syrinx, or panpipe, which he is said to have invented; especially associated with Arcadia.

Panopeus. Town in Phocis in central Greece, home of Harpalycos, Heracles' instructor in boxing and wrestling.
Paphian. Another name for Aphrodite, from Paphos, a center of her worship in Cyprus.
Paris. Son of Priam, king of Troy, whose abduction of Helen of Sparta, wife of Menelaos, brought about the Trojan war.
Parnassos. Mountain near Delphi in central Greece, sacred to Apollo and the Muses.
Paros, Parian. Island in the Aegean, one of the Cyclades; famous for its marble.
Patroclos. Great friend of Achilles, who in the Trojan war was killed by Hector while wearing Achilles' armor.
Pelasgian. Pertaining to the pre-Dorian inhabitants of Greece.
Peleus. Father of Achilles by Thetis, a sea nymph; his father, Aiacos, expelled him from Aegina for killing his half brother; fled to Thessaly and became king of Phthia.
Peloponnesos, Peloponnesian. The large southern peninsula of Greece below the Gulf of Corinth; in Id. 15, the reference is to the Doric dialect of the Greek language.
Pelops. Son of Tantalos, father of Atreus, and grandfather of Agamemnon and Menelaos; the Peloponnesos ("island of Pelops") was named for him.
Peneios. River in Thessaly in northeastern Greece, which flows through the Vale of Tempe into the Aegean; Larissa is situated on its south bank.
Pentheus. Agave's son, king of Thebes, who is torn to pieces by maenads for spying on their rites in their worship of Dionysos.
Perimede. A sorceress, possibly another name for Medea.
Persephone. Daughter of Demeter and Zeus, who was abducted by Hades and spends the winter season as his queen in the underworld region of the dead and the spring and summer, as a goddess of vegetation, on earth with her mother.
Perseus. Son of Zeus and Danaë and the ancestor of Alcmene and Heracles; with the help of Athene and Hermes, he slew the Gorgon Medusa, and married Andromeda, an Ethiopian princess, after rescuing her from a sea monster.
Persia. Area from the Hellespont to the Indus River conquered by Alexander the Great.
Phaëthon. Son of Helios, the sun god; in Id. 25, a white bull sacred to Helios.
Phalaros. In Id. 5, a ram.
Phasis. River in Colchis, at the eastern end of the Black Sea.
Philammon. In Id. 24, father of Eumolpos, Heracles' music instructor.

Philinos. In Id. 2, an athlete skilled in running; in Id. 7, the youth loved by Aratos in Simichidas's song.

Philista. In Id. 2, a flute girl.

Philitas. A poet of the third century B.C., a native of Cos and tutor of Ptolemy Philadelphus.

Philoitios. In the *Odyssey*, a faithful cowherd who helps Odysseus kill Penelope's suitors.

Philondas. In Id. 4, an owner of cattle; in Id. 5, a friend of Lacon.

Phoebus. Another name for Apollo.

Phoenicia. Country of seafarers and traders in southwestern Asia at the eastern end of the Mediterranean (now Syria and Lebanon), whose principal cities were Tyre and Sidon; it established many colonies in the western Mediterranean, among them Carthage.

Pholos. A Centaur to whom Dionysos, repaying a favor, gave a jar of wine, to be opened only when Heracles arrived, generations later—an occasion that turned into a riot that resulted in his death and the death of Cheiron.

Phoroneus. Legendary king of Argos and ancester of the Argives.

Phrasidamos. In Id. 7, the friend at whose farm Simichidas celebrates the harvest festival.

Phrygia. Region in central Asia Minor (now Turkey), northeast of the Aiolian and Ionian Greek settlements along the coast; in Id. 15, a nursemaid, probably a Phrygian slave.

Phyleus. Son of Augeias, king of Elis, to whom Heracles relates the story of the Nemean lion.

Physcos. In Id. 4, apparently a landowner in the vicinity of Croton in southeastern Italy.

Pieria. Region north of Mt. Olympus in northeastern Greece inhabited by the Muses.

Pindos. Mountains in northwestern Greece.

Pisa. City on the Alpheus River near Olympia in the western Peloponnesos.

Pleiades. A cluster of stars in the constellation Taurus, representing the seven daughters of Atlas, who were changed into stars.

Plutos. God of agricultural wealth; son of Demeter and Iasion.

Polybotas. In Id. 10, master of the flute girl Bucaios loves.

Polydeuces (also called Pollux). Son of Leda and Tyndareos (or Zeus), twin brother of Castor, and brother of Helen of Sparta; a notable boxer; one of the company of heroes who sailed in the *Argo* to recover the Golden Fleece; although immortal, he begged to share Castor's fate, and exchanges his immortality for death every other day.

Polyphemos. The Cyclops, a one-eyed monster, son of Poseidon and the sea nymph Thoösa, whom Odysseus encountered in Sicily on his voyage home to Ithaca after the Trojan war and blinded; in love with the sea nymph Galatea.

Pontos. The Black Sea; Colchis, the destination of the *Argo*, was at its eastern extremity.

Poseidon. God of the sea, of horses, and of earthquakes; brother of Zeus and Hades, usually depicted carrying the three-pronged trident; father of the Cyclops Polyphemos and, in Id. 22, of Amycos, king of the Bebryces.

Praxinoë. In Id. 15, a housewife of Alexandria.

Praxiteles. In Id. 5, probably a local craftsman rather than the famous sculptor of the same name.

Priam. King of Troy at the time of the Trojan war; father of Hector and Paris.

Priapos. God of fertility of gardens and herds.

Propontis. The Sea of Marmara, connected with the Aegean by the Dardanelles (Hellespont) and with the Black Sea by the Bosporus.

Proteus. Ancient god of the sea who lived in a cave and herded seals; he was able to assume many forms at will.

Ptelea. In Id. 7, apparently a winegrowing area of Cos.

Pterelaos. An enemy of Electryon whom Amphitryon vanquished in battle, thus winning Alcmene in marriage.

Ptolemy I (Soter) (d. 283 B.C.). One of the three Macedonian generals who divided Alexander's empire after his death; king of Egypt, 305–283 B.C.; son of Lagos of Macedonia and father of Ptolemy Philadelphus, with whom he shared the last two years of his reign; deified after death. His capital, Alexandria, was the cultural center of the Hellenistic world, noted especially for its great library, which he founded.

Ptolemy II (Philadelphus) (309–246 B.C.). Son of Ptolemy I and Berenicë; king of Egypt, 285–246 B.C.; continued his father's policy of military conquest with the able assistance of his sister and second wife, Arsinoë II, and with generous patronage extended the influence of Alexandria as the cultural center of the world.

Pylos. City in the southwestern Peloponnesos ruled by Neleus and, later, his son Nestor.

Pyrrhos. Son of Achilles, also called Neoptolemos, who was summoned to Troy after his father's death and helped end the war by bringing Philoctetes to the siege; killed Priam and was awarded Hector's wife, Andromache, as a slave; married Hermione, daughter of Helen and Menelaos, and was killed by Orestes, son of Agamemnon and Clytemnestra.

Pyrrhos. A poet and musician popular in Alexandria in Theocritus's time.

Pythagorean. A follower of the philosopher Pythagoras, who founded a school and settlement in Croton, in southeastern Italy; its members were ascetics, especially in the matter of food.

Pyxa. Town on the island of Cos.

Rhea. Ancient earth goddess, wife of Cronos and mother of Zeus, Hera, Poseidon, Demeter, and the other Olympian gods who overthrew the Titans; identified with Cybele, the Great Mother of Asia Minor.

Rhenea. Small island near Delos in the central Aegean; one of the Cyclades.

Rhodope. Mountains in Thrace, now Bulgaria.

Samos. Island in the Aegean off the west coast of Turkey, north of Cos.

Sardinia. Large island in the Mediterranean northwest of Sicily.

Satyrs. Goatlike creatures of the woodland associated with Pan.

Scopas. A king of Thessaly in the fifth century B.C., whose capital was Crannon; a patron of Simonides.

Scythia. Region northeast of the Black Sea inhabited by nomads.

Selene. The moon goddess, another aspect of Artemis; also associated with Hecate; for love of Endymion, a beautiful Carian youth, she bestowed on him immortality and perpetual youth in the form of eternal sleep.

Semele. Daughter of Cadmos, founder of Thebes; mother of Dionysos, destroyed by lightning before his birth by the sight of her lover, Zeus, in his immortal form.

Semiramis. Legendary queen of Babylon.

Sibyrtas. In Id. 5, a landowner of Thurii in southeastern Italy; master of Lacon.

Sicelidas. A poet of the third century B.C., more commonly called Asclepiades.

Sicily. Large island in the Mediterranean south of Italy, colonized by Greeks around the eighth century B.C.

Simaitha. In Id. 2, a lovesick girl who casts a spell to win back her faithless lover.

Simichidas. In Id. 7, a poet who attends a harvest festival; thought to be Theocritus.

Simoeis. River near Troy in northwestern Asia Minor (now Turkey), a tributary of the Scamander.

Simos. In Id. 14, a friend of Aischinas.

Sparta. City in Laconia in the southern Peloponnesos, situated on the Eurotas River; home of Helen and Menelaos.

Sybaris. Greek city in southeastern Italy notorious for its luxury and licentiousness; also a nearby river and lake of the same name.
Syracuse. Greek city in eastern Sicily, founded in the eighth century B.C. by Archias of Corinth; thought to be the birthplace of Theocritus.
Syria. Country in southwestern Asia comprising modern Syria, Lebanon, Israel, and Jordan.

Teiresias. Blind seer who figures in many of the legends concerning Thebes.
Telamon. In Id. 13, Heracles' rowing companion aboard the *Argo* and tablemate ashore; son of Aiacos, exiled from Aegina with his brother, Peleus; king of Salamis and father of Ajax, a hero of the Trojan war.
Telemos. A prophet who in the *Odyssey* predicted the fate of Polyphemos.
Tempe. Valley between Mts. Ossa and Olympus in northeastern Thessaly where the Peneios River enters the Aegean.
Thebes. City in Boeotia in central Greece, founded by Cadmos of Phoenicia, whose daughter Semele was the mother of Dionysos; kingdom of Oedipus and birthplace of Heracles.
Theseus. Hero of Athenian legend, who, among other adventures, vanquished the Minotaur with Ariadne's assistance and escaped with her from Crete, abandoning her on the voyage home.
Thessaly, Thessalian. Large region in northeastern Greece south of Macedonia; especially famous for its horses.
Thestios. King of Sparta and father of Leda.
Thestylis. In Id. 2, Simaitha's slave girl.
Thetis. A sea nymph, mother of Achilles.
Theugenis. Wife of Nicias, a physician, poet, and friend of Theocritus who lived in Miletos; Theocritus gave her an ivory distaff accompanied by a poem.
Theumaridas. In Id. 2, a friend of Simaitha.
Thrace, Thracian. Region in eastern Europe extending south to the Sea of Marmara, east to the Black Sea, and north to the Danube River, now divided among Greece, Bulgaria, and Turkey; a remote and barbarous region to the Greeks, especially those of Alexandria and the southern Aegean.
Thurii. Greek city in southeastern Italy, founded in the fifth century B.C. near the former site of Sybaris, which had earlier been destroyed by Croton.
Thybris. In Id. 1, apparently a mountain in Sicily, perhaps another name for Etna.
Thyonichos. In Id. 14, a friend of Aischinas.

Thyrsis. In Id. 1, a Sicilian shepherd and singer.
Timagetos. In Id. 2, proprietor of a wrestling school, or palaestra.
Tiryns. City in the northeastern Peloponnesos near Mycenae and Argos; its king, Eurystheus, exacted twelve labors of Heracles.
Tityos. A giant who offered violence to Leto and was killed by Apollo and Artemis and cast into Tartaros, where his body covered nine acres and vultures fed on his liver.
Tityros. In Id. 3, a goatherd; in Id. 7, a singer.
Trachis. Town in Thessaly on the Malian Gulf opposite the northwestern tip of the island of Euboea; home of Heracles at the time of his death.
Trinacria. Another name for Sicily, so called because of its three capes.
Triopium. Promontory on the southwestern coast of Turkey across from Cos, the site of ancient Cnidos, now Cape Crio; a Dorian settlement founded by the legendary Triopas.
Troy. City in northwestern Asia Minor (now Turkey) near the entrance to the Hellespont (Dardanelles), against which the Greeks waged war for ten years; Priam was its king.
Tydeus. A native of Calydon, exiled for homicide, who took refuge with King Adrastos of Argos and married his daughter Deïpyle; father of Diomedes, a hero of the Trojan war; took part in the expedition against Thebes and was killed there.
Tyndareos. King of Sparta; husband of Leda; father of Helen, Castor, Polydeuces, and Clytemnestra; half brother of Aphareus and Leucippos. Leda, his wife, was seduced by Zeus in the form of a swan, and therefore Helen and Polydeuces were only nominally his children.

Xenea. In Id. 7, the girl for whom Daphnis died of love.

Zacynthos. Island off the northwestern coast of the Peloponnesos. In Id. 4, the reference is obscure; perhaps the name of an inhabitant of Croton.
Zeus. Chief of the Olympian gods, all-knowing and all-powerful; son of Cronos and Rhea; god of the earth, rain, and justice, who punishes wrongdoers with the thunderbolt and wears the aegis, a goatskin breastplate, which his daughter Athene also wears; husband of Hera, his sister, and father of countless children, both human and divine.
Zopyrion. In Id. 15, Praxinoë's son.